IS CHRISTIE STEALING BETH'S BOYFRIEND?

"Keith asked me if I'd go to the movies with him," Christie said. "It's okay with you, isn't it, Beth? I only gave him a tentative yes. I won't do it if you don't want me to."

Beth's face felt as if it had been starched stiff when she tried to smile. "Oh. Oh, no. That's okay. I said you could date him."

"Good," responded Christie, looking genuinely relieved. "I really didn't *think* you'd mind. Especially after you said you were going to break up with Keith anyway. Actually it might make it easier for you to break up with him if I do go out with him."

"I hadn't thought of that," said Beth, putting on her best acting face.

THE FABULOUS FIVE

Playing the Part

Betsy Haynes

BANTAM BOOKS
NEW YORK · TORONTO · LONDON · SYDNEY · AUCKLAND

RL 5, 009-012

PLAYING THE PART

A Bantam Skylark Book / July 1989

*Skylark Books is a registered trademark of Bantam Books, a division of
Bantam Doubleday Dell Publishing Group, Inc.
Registered in U.S. Patent and Trademark Office and elsewhere.*

ISBN 0-553-15745-0

Published simultaneously in the United States and Canada

Bantam Books are published by Bantam Books, a division of Bantam Doubleday Dell Publishing Group, Inc. Its trademark, consisting of the words
"Bantam Books" and the portrayal of a rooster, is Registered in U.S. Patent
and Trademark Office and in other countries. Marca Registrada. Bantam
Books, 666 Fifth Avenue, New York, New York 10103.

Playing the
Part

CHAPTER

1

"I really can't help it, Keith," Beth Barry said in frustration. "I've got cheerleading practice tomorrow after school, and then I've got to study for the play tryouts. You know how important getting the part of Julie in the school play is to me."

Keith Masterson, Beth's boyfriend, had been complaining for weeks about her being so busy she didn't have time to see him. And now she had just told him she was trying out for a part in the play, and she would have to spend more of her evenings studying the script.

"What's more important, me or the play?" he

1

grumbled. He was slouched angrily on the opposite end of the couch.

"You're important to me. You know that. How long have we been going together? Since sixth grade, right? Doesn't that tell you something?"

"It tells me you may be getting tired of me," he responded with a sour look on his face.

"That's not so," she said, moving closer and taking his hand. "I like you better than any other boy." She leaned against him and put her head on his shoulder. "I mean it."

She looked into his eyes as his strong arms wrapped around her, and she felt herself going limp as he drew her closer. A tingling sensation ran up and down her back, and she started to close her eyes in anticipation of his kiss.

"WAHOO! WE CAUGHT YOU!"

Beth jerked, bumping her mouth on Keith's and splitting her lip. Alicia, Beth's five-year-old sister, jumped on Keith's back and puckered her lips at Beth. "We caught you smoochin'! I'm gonna tell."

Beth shot her little sister a dirty look, then turned to glare at her brother Todd. The fifth-grader was standing in front of the couch holding his sponge-rubber football and grinning at Beth and Keith. Agatha, the family sheepdog, sat next to him with a silly look on her face, as if she knew what was going on. Beth stuck her tongue out at both her brother and the dog.

"Hey, Keith, how about some football?" Todd asked, throwing the ball at him.

"Okay, partner," Keith responded, getting up and tossing the ball back.

Beth's heart sank. In less than one second, they had gone from a big love scene to a football game in her family room. She'd almost had Keith convinced that she wasn't trying to avoid him with excuses about having to study for the play, cheerleading practice, and her parents getting tougher on school studies because she was out so much doing other things. It wasn't fair. You couldn't do anything in this house without someone butting in.

"Get out of here, you two," she yelled at Alicia and Todd. "Can't a person have any privacy around here?"

"Catch," said Todd, tossing the ball to her. It hit her in the nose. "You and Alicia against me and Keith in a game of touch."

"Not fair! Not fair!" screamed Alicia. "Me and Keith against you and Bethy."

"Boys against girls," yelled Todd.

"Okay," said Keith, smiling and winking at Beth. "Why don't we let the girls have the ball first?"

"Aw, nuts," Todd said under his breath.

Beth frowned back at Keith but resigned herself to

humoring them. She and Alicia huddled at one end of the room, and Agatha stuck her head in between them to get attention.

"Okay, Alicia. You hike the ball to me and run to the fireplace, and I'll throw you a pass," Beth said, pushing Agatha's head away.

"What will Agafa do?" asked Alicia.

"Oh, she'll block Todd. Go on, hike it to me when I say the number two."

Alicia bent over the ball, and Beth started to count as she had seen the Wakeman Junior High quarterback do. "Hut! One! Two!"

Alicia centered the ball, and it rolled on the floor toward Beth. Todd tried to run around Alicia and tripped over Agatha.

"Darn dog!" he yelled.

Alicia reached the end of the room, but Keith was waiting for her there. Beth quickly stepped around Todd, who was scrambling toward her on his hands and knees, and ran toward the fireplace goal.

Keith dashed forward and grabbed Beth, pulling her to the floor. She could feel his arms holding her gently as she went down and knew that he was trying not to hurt her. He came down half on top of her, and Todd piled on his back. Agatha was jumping around and barking, and Alicia was yelling, "No fair! No fair!"

At the bottom of the pileup, Beth saw a twinkle in

Keith's eyes as he held her. He was like his old self again. "There's always a way to get close if I try hard enough," he said with a laugh. Beth smiled back at him.

"Has anybody seen my fingernail polish?" Brittany asked as she walked into the room. Brittany was Beth's sixteen-year-old sister. "Oh, gross. What are you doing piled up like that? Alicia, Mom told me to tell you it's time for bed." They peeled off the pile one by one, and Keith took Beth's hands and pulled her up.

"I've got to go," Keith said. "Coach wants us in bed by eleven, and you know I always do what I'm told."

They walked out to the front porch with their arms around each other's waist. Beth quickly checked the windows to see if Alicia was peeking.

"Are you sure I can't come over tomorrow night?" he asked.

"You know I've got a cheerleaders' meeting tomorrow night," she answered.

"Wednesday, then?"

"That's the meeting for the school play. Mr. Levine will be giving out the scripts. Kaci Davis, Taffy Sinclair, Laura McCall, and I are all trying out for the part of Julie, the female lead."

"How much of your time is the school play going to take?" he said, scowling again.

"I don't know. If I luck out and get the lead role, quite a bit I guess. Practice will be on Mondays, Wednesdays, and Fridays after school, and I'm going to have to practice like mad this week to even get the part."

Keith looked down. "And you've got cheerleading practice on Tuesdays and Thursdays. That doesn't leave *any* time for us," he complained.

"But this acting part is important to me," she said, trying to make him understand. "This will be my first chance to star in a junior high play, and Mr. Levine said that he has a friend who's a casting director on Broadway. He's coming to visit and will be at the tryouts." She looked up hopefully at Keith, but he was still frowning. He just didn't understand.

"Don't be mad," she said, putting a finger on each corner of his mouth and pushing it into a smile. "We can still be together a lot."

"When?" asked Keith. "Between midnight and six A.M.? I don't think you even want to go steady."

"That's not funny," she said, making a pouty face. "I'll see you at school every day, and we can go out on Friday and Saturday nights. We'll still see a lot of each other."

"Maybe," Keith answered.

Beth looked at him closely. He seemed so angry about it. Why would a little part in a play make him mad?

"You'll see," she said, trying to sound perky. "We'll have lots of dates." She stood on her toes and kissed him on the nose. "Don't be such a grouch. Smile."

She moved close and wrapped her arms around his neck. Standing on her tiptoes, she kissed him. His body was rigid, and he didn't put his arms around her. It was like kissing a dead fish.

Beth's anger flared. "Okay, be that way. I think you're the one who doesn't want to go steady, and that's just fine with me!" She slammed the door behind her as she stormed into the house.

CHAPTER

"Taffy, Kaci, and Laura?" said Jana Morgan as The Fabulous Five gathered at their favorite spot by the school fence before school the next morning. "Those are three tough girls you're going up against for the lead role in the play, Beth. Besides modeling, Taffy's done professional acting on television; Kaci thinks she's the queen of Wacko Junior High; and Laura is convinced she can do anything. I don't envy you trying to beat them out for the part, especially Taffy."

"I know it will be tough," said Beth, "but don't forget that I've read tons of books on acting, and I was in all the school plays at Mark Twain Elementary. Besides, Mr. Levine said he has a friend, whose name is Mr. Stapleton, who will be at the tryouts. He's a casting director from New York City. Maybe he'll notice me."

"You can do it," said Katie. "We'll help."

"That's right," said Christie. "We'll help you practice as much as you need us to. Just the way all of you did for me when I was trying out for the Super Quiz team."

"We'll do anything you need," joined in Melanie.

Jana Morgan, Katie Shannon, Christie Winchell, and Melanie Edwards were Beth's four best friends and members of The Fabulous Five. The five of them had been best friends since they went to Mark Twain Elementary School together. They had even stayed close after starting at Wakeman Junior High and getting involved in different activities.

"Dahlings, it's so nice of you to offer to help little old me," Beth said in her most dramatic voice. The others rocked on their heels with laughter.

"But hark! I think I hear my fans calling," she said, putting a hand up to her ear. "Or is that Taffy, Kaci, and Laura crying because they know I'll get to play Julie?" Melanie doubled over with laughter, and Jana and Katie leaned on each other for support.

"Enough! Enough!" said Christie, holding her sides. "I can't stand it."

"Look who's watching us," said Katie, nodding toward the school.

Beth turned and saw Laura McCall and her friends Tammy Lucero, Melissa McConnell, and Funny Hawthorne staring at them. The four of them were a rival clique that had gone to Riverfield Elementary and called themselves The Fantastic Foursome. They were always trying to outdo The Fabulous Five.

Beth put her hand up to her mouth as if she were telling a secret and said in a loud whisper, "I'll bet they think we're talking about them, don't you?"

Laura frowned at her, and Beth knew that was exactly what she thought.

"Is it true that the play you're trying out for is about Romeo and Juliet going to school at Wacko Junior High?" asked Melanie.

"Well, sort of. Mr. Levine has rewritten *Romeo and Juliet* and named the characters Ronnie and Julie. They go to Wakeman, and their parents are mad at each other and won't let Julie and Ronnie date," explained Beth.

"That's the saddest thing I've ever heard," said Melanie with a little sigh.

"Wait until I finish telling you about it. It gets kind of funny. Ronnie sneaks over to Julie's house late one night to borrow her homework. Her parents come home, and Julie puts Ronnie in a hall closet to hide because they'll be mad if they find him there. Her mom and dad hang around and don't go to bed, and Julie can't figure out how to get Ronnie out of the closet so he can go home."

"Oh, no," gasped Christie.

"Well, it turns out his parents have found out he's not in his room and they go out looking for him," continued Beth. "They spot his bike outside Julie's house and knock on the door. Julie gets into the closet to talk to Ronnie while both sets of parents are arguing, and she closes the door. When the adults look for her, they can't find her either, and they start worrying that she's run off to be with him."

"Eeek," squealed Jana. "What happens next?"

Beth's friends were looking at her in anticipation.

"Julie and Ronnie are afraid to come out of the closet and stay there while the parents are arguing," Beth said, enjoying the looks on their faces. "In the end the parents are so worried about the kids that they make up. When Julie and Ronnie finally sneak back out of the closet, the parents are so happy to see them they tell them they can date."

"You mean Julie gets to spend all that time in the closet with Ronnie?" asked Melanie. "That's cool. No wonder you want to play the part. Who's playing the part of Ronnie?"

"I don't know. He hasn't been cast yet, but there are some cute guys trying out—Chet Miller and Garrett Boldt."

"Chet's a ninth-grader," said Christie.

"And really cute," added Jana.

"I'll be so jealous if Garrett gets the part and you get to kiss him onstage," said Melanie. "I'm the one who likes him."

"If they left out all the boys you like, there would be no one left to try out for the play," said Katie.

Melanie stuck her nose up at her friend.

"Is there really kissing in the play?" asked Jana.

Beth nodded.

"I'd be embarrassed to kiss Randy in front of an audience," Jana said.

"What will Keith say if you have to kiss some other guy in front of everyone?" asked Melanie. "Won't he be jealous?"

Beth thought about the argument that Keith and she had had the night before, and her anger at him returned. "There's no reason for him to be jealous," she said with an air of assurance. "After all, it's just acting, and professional actresses have to kiss good-looking guys all the time. It's part of the job. Besides, he's mad at me anyway."

"What's he mad at you for?" asked Christie.

"He's mad because I'm so busy and can't see him every time he wants to. He thinks I ought to be around for him all the time. He'll get over it."

"But what if he doesn't?" asked Jana. "Is the play worth it?"

"You bet it is. It's kind of like your breaking up

with Jon, Christie. Keith doesn't understand that there are things that are important to me besides dating and watching him play football." Beth's own words surprised her. She hadn't realized how strongly she felt about things until now as she explained it to her friends.

"That's a very liberated attitude," said Katie. Then grinning, she added, "Maybe there's hope for you after all."

"But do you *really* feel that way?" asked Christie.

"Sure I do," Beth declared. "I wouldn't say so if I didn't, would I?"

"What if Keith asked someone else for a date?" asked Melanie. "Wouldn't that just kill you?"

Beth let out a big laugh, trying to appear unconcerned. "He could date anyone he wants."

Her friends looked at her doubtfully, but before Beth could repeat what she'd just said, the bell rang. As she followed her friends inside the school building, she couldn't help wishing that she could take back what she'd just said.

Beth saw Keith in the hallways several times between morning classes, and each time he looked away. The first time he did it, she was confused. In the past when they had argued, they had always made up pretty quickly. Why was he so angry this time? When Keith ignored her again, Beth was furious. If he wants to be that way, she thought, well, let him.

For good measure, she hurried out of her English class in the afternoon and leaned against the wall. The classroom was next door to Keith's class, and usually the first one out waited for the other. Then they'd walk together to their next classes.

Beth was prepared when he came out the door. She stuck her nose into the air and sailed right in front of him without speaking. There! she thought. That ought to put Keith Masterson in his place. Maybe now he would realize just how foolish their argument had been. She giggled to herself. Besides, it would be fun when they made up.

CHAPTER

"*O*kay, everybody," Mr. Levine said. "We've got enough scripts for everyone who's going to try out " He stood on the stage in the auditorium Wednesday after school, surrounded by kids who were waving their hands and asking for scripts. "When I call your name, come up and get one, and I'll check you off. And please tell me which part you're interested in so I can make sure I've got you down for the right one."

"Shawnie Pendergast." Beth watched Shawnie weave her way through the crowd to get her script. Shawnie is really making an effort to be friendly since she ran away and almost got Katie in trouble, she thought.

"Garrett Boldt," called Mr. Levine. "Taffy Sinclair."

Beth's apprehension grew as Taffy held up her hand and walked confidently over to Mr. Levine to get her script. Taffy looked as if she belonged on a stage. She may have all that experience, Beth told herself, but she doesn't want the part as much as I do.

"Kaci Davis." Beth felt a twinge of worry as she watched Kaci move to get her script. Beth couldn't help noticing again how pretty Kaci was. And she was a ninth-grader. How much chance does a seventh-grader have against a ninth-grader? she thought.

"Laura McCall."

Tall Laura, with the long blond braid that started on the top of her head and hung down over her shoulder, moved through the crowd of kids like a queen. She's pretty, too, but I look more like the person who should be playing the part of Julie, Beth thought.

"Beth Barry."

Beth squared her shoulders, held her chin high, and imagined that she was a great actress going up to receive her script for a new starring role. She knew everyone was watching her. I'll show them, she told herself. They haven't seen acting yet, until they've seen Beth Barry act.

"Okay, everyone," Mr. Levine announced. "Tryouts are on Friday after school. Those who are chosen can keep their scripts to practice with. Those who aren't chosen can return the scripts to me later. Lots of luck to all of you."

Beth squeezed the script tightly to her body as she left the auditorium. This was her first junior high script, and it seemed so grown-up. For the first time in her life, she felt as if she were really on her way to becoming an actress.

That evening, after Beth had helped clean up the dinner dishes, she was on her way to her room to study when the phone rang just as she was passing it.

She grabbed it at the same instant that Alicia came running in and Brittany appeared in the other doorway with an it's-obviously-for-me look.

"Beth?" It was Christie.

"Oh, hi, Christie," Beth answered. She shrugged at Brittany and gave her sister a fake smile.

Christie talked about school for a moment, but Beth could tell that that wasn't what was on her mind.

Finally Christie said, "Um, Beth. Do you remember when we were talking, and you said that you didn't care who Keith dated?"

"Yes," said Beth, but little tingles of apprehension were racing up her spine.

"Um, well, I was just wondering . . ."

"Wondering what?" asked Beth. She heard Christie take a deep breath.

"Well, I saw Keith right after school. You know, when you were at the meeting for the play. And he sort of asked me to go to Bumpers with him. I was shocked that he asked, and naturally I didn't want to butt into your romance, so I said no. But I was wondering if you really meant what you said about not caring if Keith dated other girls." Her voice trailed off to just above a whisper.

Beth's mouth dropped open. Keith had asked Christie to go to Bumpers. Bumpers was the fast-food restaurant where *everyone* hung out after school. How could he do a thing like that? Was he trying to show her that he could do without her? She had just been talking big the other day and had definitely expected to make up with him, but if he felt *that* way, she would just show him.

"You should have said yes," she said firmly. "It wouldn't make the slightest bit of difference to me." She flipped her hand casually, as if Christie could see it over the phone. "Just like you, Christie, now and then I need a little space. I've got *so* much going on that I want to be involved in. Maybe it's time we didn't go steady anymore."

"If you say so," said Christie.

Beth smiled to herself after they had hung up. Despite what Christie had told her, Beth didn't think for one minute that Keith would really go out with someone else, especially not with one of Beth's best friends. He was just trying to make her angry because she wouldn't spend as much time with him as he wanted her to.

Back in her room, Beth grabbed the script and flipped through the pages. Then she tossed it onto the bed and opened her social studies book instead.

She had read only two paragraphs when her thoughts drifted back to Keith and Christie. What Christie had said about Keith's asking her to go to Bumpers was really bugging her.

She had known that Keith was upset at her for being so busy, but she couldn't believe he'd ask Christie to go to Bumpers with him. How could he do that to her? Was he really that mad at her? Didn't he know how important the play was to her? Maybe if she called him and talked to him again, he would understand.

She got out of her chair and took two steps toward the door. No, she thought, I can't do that. I have pride. Keith was the one who didn't understand her. It was up to him to call. In fact, he would probably call her this very evening. When he did, she would just pretend there was nothing wrong.

She walked back to her desk and sat down. A second later she leapt up again and opened the door. Was that the telephone ringing? She could hear Brittany talking to someone on the phone downstairs. She waited a minute to see if Brittany would call her, but the conversation continued, and she knew it was one of Brittany's friends. She left the door open a crack so she could hear if the phone rang again.

Beth walked over to the bed and picked up the play script. She was dying to start practicing, but first she had to study for her social studies test.

For the next fifteen minutes Beth tried to study, but instead she could only stare into space. If Keith asks Christie to go to Bumpers with him again, would Christie accept? she wondered. I'll die if they go out and everyone sees them together.

What if Keith asked Christie to go to the movies with him on Friday night? Would she go?

No! Beth thought emphatically. Christie was one of her best friends. She wouldn't go on a date with Keith, she thought smugly. Best friends didn't date each other's boyfriends, and Christie and Beth had been best friends for a long time. Besides, Keith would get over his anger soon.

But with a sinking feeling Beth remembered what she had told Christie and everyone else in The Fabulous Five: She didn't care about Keith; she was thinking about breaking up anyway. Why did I say such a stupid thing? she thought. I didn't mean that seriously. Christie ought to know that. She ought to understand that I was just talking big again.

Beth sighed. Her big mouth was always getting her into trouble. One of the worst times had been when she had told The Fantastic Foursome that she was going to have a party that was bigger and better than the one Laura McCall was having. Then she had gotten grounded and couldn't have any kind of party, even a teensy one. Then she had told everyone that Jana was related to Trevor Morgan, the lead singer with the rock group Brain Damage. Christie should know by now that Beth was always saying things that she didn't mean.

Beth glanced over again at the script lying in the middle of her bed. As long as she was having difficulty reading her social studies book, she would make a deal with herself. She would read a little bit of the script, and then she would come back to her social studies until she was sure she knew enough to make an A on the test.

That's fair, she thought happily. She picked up the script and flopped on the bed and began thumbing through the pages, counting the lines for Julie's part. Gosh, there are a lot of words, she thought, and started reading out loud.

"Oh, Ronnie, I do so want to date you, but you know how my parents feel."

Beth liked the sound of her voice, but it just wasn't quite right. She tried speaking the part again, this time louder and with more power. That's better, she thought excitedly, but I can do it even better.

Beth went to her bookcase and picked out one of her books on acting and reread the parts she had underlined. *Calm yourself by warming up. . . . Try to show that extra spark. . . . Find the spotlight and keep your head up and your face forward. . . . Speak loudly and slowly.*

Beth giggled at the suggestion below the last one. It said you should try reading your part to someone else through a door. The idea was to help you to speak your lines loudly and clearly enough to be heard in the last row. Maybe she ought to try reading to her brother Brian through his door. If he could hear her with his stereo turned up, anyone in the auditorium should be able to hear her without a microphone.

Concentrate on your lines. Try to become the person you are portraying.

Beth thought about that for a moment. It made sense. If you were going to act as if you were someone else, you should really try to forget yourself and be that person. If you tried hard enough, and concentrated, you could be *anyone* you wanted to be. I can make people think I'm happy when I'm not or mad when I'm happy, if I really want to, she thought. I can hide my real feelings and play whatever part I choose. I'm not just an actress, I'm a good one!

"Okay," she said out loud. "Just call me Julie because that's who I am."

She bent over and touched her toes ten times and did some stretches and deep-breathing exercises. Then she opened her closet door so she could see herself in the full-length mirror and tried reading the part again. This time, the words rolled off her lips, and she made grand gestures at the mirror with her hands as if she were speaking to someone. Beth smiled at her reflection, bowed, and pretended that she could hear the audience applauding.

Then a thought came to her, and she went into her closet. The music from Brian's stereo was vibrating the walls, even though it was supposed to be turned down so that everybody else could do their homework. The lid of the trunk where she kept her acting things screeched as Beth opened it.

First she pulled out Brian's gorilla costume and put it on the floor. Then came the Oriental fans, wigs, and fake mustaches. Finally, she found the makeup kit and took it back to her desk.

Spreading the contents out on top of her books, Beth grabbed a bottle of foundation and opened it. After she'd spread a layer over her face, she dusted powder over it. Then she contoured her face with a dark blush and carefully edged her eyes with liner. Next she put on a bright red lipstick and darkened her eyebrows with a pencil.

My hair, she thought, running her fingers through it. She dug her brush out of her purse and tried to comb her short, spiky hair into different styles. Oh, well, she said to herself, there's not much I can do with it. Finally she patted it into place.

She spun in front of the mirror and looked at herself from all sides. She almost looked the part already.

Beth picked up the script and started reading again, this time from the very first line. She concentrated and really tried to feel like Julie.

Soon the image in the mirror that had looked like Beth Barry faded, and she saw Julie standing in front of her. Her voice got more dramatic and her movements more eloquent. Time passed without her realizing it as she read through the whole play.

When Beth was finished, she felt totally exhausted. She lay down on her bed with the script clutched to her chest and thought about what it would be like to be a big star. With visions of herself as the lead in a Broadway play, taking bows as the audience applauded wildly, she finally drifted off to sleep.

CHAPTER

*B*eth woke with a start. The lamp next to her bed was still on, and sunlight was streaming into her room. The social studies book was lying unopened on her desk.

"Oh, my gosh, the test!" she said, jumping out of bed.

She ran to the closet mirror and stared in horror at her face. The makeup was all smudged and she looked like some kind of monster. She grabbed a handful of tissues and scrubbed her face until it was sore and red but finally clean.

Picking up her social studies book, she headed for

the bathroom. When she got there, the door was closed.

"Hurry up and let someone else use the bathroom!" she called, knocking sharply on the door.

"You can wait your turn!" Brittany's voice came from inside.

Beth bounced up and down, anxiously waiting to get in. She flipped her book open and skimmed the pages.

"Can I go in next, Bethy?" asked Alicia, coming out of her room and walking with her legs crossed. "I've got to go to the bathroom."

Beth rolled her eyes to the ceiling and knocked on the door again. "Brittany, will you hurry? We've got an emergency out here. Alicia has to go to the bathroom."

Mumbled words that Beth couldn't understand came from inside.

Alicia jumped up and down, and Beth began to worry that she really wouldn't be able to wait.

"BRITTANY!" she yelled, knocking on the door harder.

The door popped open and Brittany emerged, throwing a towel over her shoulder as Alicia slipped past her.

"All right, all ready!" said Brittany. "I'll be glad when I go to college and don't have to share the bathroom with so many people."

"College has thousands of people," retorted Beth.

"But I won't be sharing a bathroom with all of them," Brittany hurled back over her shoulder.

She's got a point, thought Beth, opening her book again.

She felt a paw hitting the back of her leg, and turned to see Agatha smiling up at her. "You will have to wait your turn," she told the dog. Agatha's smile seemed to grow at the attention.

Finally Beth heard the toilet flush, and Alicia came out. She yelled, "Thanks, Bethy!" as she ran back to her room.

Inside the bathroom, Beth propped her book against the mirror and began reading and brushing her teeth.

"Excuse me," Beth said to Bill Soliday as she bumped into him with her tray coming out of the cafeteria line. She saw Melanie, Jana, Christie, and Katie at The Fabulous Five's regular table.

"Hi, everybody," she said as she joined them. She gave Christie an extra big smile. She didn't want Christie to think she was hurt or worried over Keith's asking her to go to Bumpers. Maybe Keith would get over being mad and wouldn't ask Christie to go to Bumpers again anyway.

"How's practice going for the tryouts?" asked Katie.

"A lot better than studying for my social studies test," answered Beth. "I didn't do very well at all. I read the assignment, but I forgot everything when I got in class."

"Have you thought about practicing your part onstage?" asked Christie. "It sure helped me before we had the tryout for the Super Quiz team. I didn't have to worry about where to be or what to do and could concentrate on the questions."

"That's a great idea!" said Beth gratefully. "I hadn't thought about that. I'll have to do it."

"Everyone's going to the football game Saturday, right?" asked Melanie. They all said yes.

"Randy said that Keith has a chance to be first in the league in yards gained," said Jana. "If he gets enough yards in Saturday's game, he'll go ahead of Mike Saharis from Georgetown Junior High."

"That's what Keith told me, too," said Christie.

"Oh, really?" said Beth. She felt her face flush and hoped Christie didn't notice.

"You didn't know that?" asked Melanie. "And he's your boyfriend."

"Uh, sure I knew that," said Beth, bluffing. "I, uh, just forgot for a minute. We haven't seen each other much lately, and I've got *so* much on my mind."

Beth tried to remember if Keith had told her about it, and she had forgotten. Was it possible that he would have said something as important as that to Christie and not told her? Don't be ridiculous, she thought angrily. Keith's *my* boyfriend. But a little voice in her head reminded her that she had said she wanted to break up with him. But she hadn't said *positively.*

It was hard for Beth to pay attention to what was going on during her afternoon classes. Her mind kept turning to Keith. She hadn't seen him all morning. Was he avoiding her? If he was mad at her, should she be the one to try and make up? That didn't seem fair because she really hadn't done anything wrong. She was just busy, that's all.

She had been on the cheerleading squad since the beginning of the school year, and he knew how much she wanted to be an actress. It was just going to take more of her time than she had expected, at least for now. She and Keith still had the weekends to date.

Did Keith think that Christie was prettier than she was? The idea shocked Beth. She hadn't thought about that before. Maybe Keith had been looking for an excuse to break up with her so that he could ask Christie for a date all along.

Beth shook her head. I'm starting to imagine things, she thought. Keith and I are just having a little argument. We've argued before, but we've never broken up.

What I have to do is take the positive approach. If I act as if nothing is wrong, everything will be all right. She straightened her back and sat up straight. It's just like playing a part in a play.

Beth pushed open the auditorium doors before cheerleading practice and walked down the aisle. She tossed her books into one of the front-row seats, and then, with her script in hand, she walked up the stairs onto the stage.

She was glad that Christie had suggested that she read her lines in the auditorium. It would seem much more real and make the tryouts easier. That's what good friends are for, she thought. They think about each other and share good ideas.

The auditorium was at least twice the size of the one at Mark Twain Elementary. Moving to the front center of the stage, she looked out over the rows of empty seats. It was awesome standing there imagining them filled with students and parents.

She took several deep breaths and pulled herself up to her full height. Arching her eyebrows, she tried to look the way she imagined a great actress would before an admiring audience.

Then, in her imagination, the applause started. It

grew and grew until it was a roar, and she could see people standing and yelling her name. An elegant man, whose face she couldn't quite see, was whistling his approval. She knew it was Mr. Stapleton, Mr. Levine's friend, the casting director from New York.

Clutching her script tightly to her chest, Beth looked out over the happy faces and smiled back her appreciation.

She opened the script and began to read the part of Julie.

CHAPTER

5

Beth and Melanie ran onto the football field to where the other cheerleaders were forming a circle around Miss Wolfe. The teacher was standing with her clipboard in hand, waiting to call roll.

Kaci Davis, who was the captain of the cheerleading squad, was standing with her hands on her hips, looking as confident as always. Taffy Sinclair stood to one side by herself, and Laura McCall was talking to Tammy Lucero, the gossip of The Fantastic Foursome.

"I see who you're looking at," said Melanie. "All of your competition is right here on this very field. Wouldn't it be something if they all sprained their ankles in cheerleading practice and couldn't go out for the play?"

Beth smiled back. "That's not too likely. You know, I think I can act better than Laura and Kaci, but how do I beat out Taffy? She's had so much experience, and she's had a lot more acting lessons than I have. She's even been on the television soap opera *Interns and Lovers*."

"I think they should declare the school play an amateur sport and not let professionals like Taffy try out," said Melanie.

"I'm sure one of the reasons she's interested is because Mr. Levine's friend, the casting director, will be here. She probably thinks there's a chance he'll offer her a big part in a Broadway play."

Beth looked at Taffy and sighed to herself. Laura and Kaci would be tough enough to beat, but did she even have a chance against Taffy?

"All right, everyvun! Listen up!" shouted Miss Wolfe. "Dekeisha Adams!"

"Here!"

"Beth Barry!"

"Here!"

Beth backed away from the group and took a pair of red-and-gold pom-pons from the pile and started warming up by bouncing on her toes and doing high kicks while Miss Wolfe continued the roll call. As she came down from a vault, she spotted Jana and

Christie walking along the edge of the field. What are they doing here? she wondered. Beth waved at them with her pom-pons. They waved back and headed to where the boys were practicing football. Jana probably has to talk to Randy about something, thought Beth. It must be important for them to interrupt practice.

"All right, girls, let's form a single line," commanded Miss Wolfe. "Ve are going to start off vith the Rock 'em cheer."

Beth and Melanie got into line next to each other and put their right legs forward and their fists together over their heads.

The practice went on for a half hour, and Beth was sweating and panting when Miss Wolfe finally let up.

"Okay, girls! Break for five minutes."

Beth and Melanie fell to the ground next to each other.

"Why do we do this to ourselves?" asked Melanie. "You know, we could be at Bumpers having a milk shake and talking to guys, but instead we're out here working our tails off."

"Most of the worthwhile guys are right here," said Beth, looking toward the area where the football team was practicing. Coach Bledsoe was giving special instruction to the line while the other players were standing around waiting.

Beth saw Jana talking to Randy, but she didn't see Keith at first. Then she spotted him near the sideline talking to Christie. They were standing close and Christie had her hand on his arm. A twinge of jealousy ran through Beth at the way they were laughing as they talked. They seemed to be enjoying each other an awful lot. Surely Christie wasn't flirting with him. Or was she?

"Tweeet!" Miss Wolfe's whistle broke into Beth's thoughts. "Okay, everyvun, back on your feet," she yelled.

During the rest of the practice, Beth followed Miss Wolfe's instructions, but she couldn't help looking over her shoulder at Keith and Christie. Twice she kicked when she should have been jumping, and she smiled apologetically at Miss Wolfe, who was starting to watch her closely.

"Could you put my pom-pons away, Beth?" asked Taffy after practice was over. "I've got to hurry. Cory's waiting for me."

"Huh?" said Beth, taking the pom-pons that Taffy shoved at her. "Uh, sure, Taffy." Beth stared after Taffy as she ran toward the sidelines where a boy was waiting.

"Isn't that Cory Dillon, the lead guitarist for the Dreadful Alternatives?" asked Melanie.

"It sure is," said Mandy McDermott. "Isn't he *gorgeous*?"

"Wow! I'll say," said Dekeisha Adams. Several other cheerleaders gathered around to stare as Taffy and Cory walked away.

"Maybe Jana won't have to worry about Taffy's trying to steal Randy from her anymore, if Taffy's dating Cory Dillon," Beth whispered to Melanie. Taffy had been trying to take Randy away from Jana since elementary school.

That evening Beth practiced for the play as she had never practiced before. She exercised until she was perspiring and tried hard to imagine she was actually Julie and how sweet and tragic it was that she and Ronnie loved each other even though their parents wouldn't let them date. Then she went over and over her lines in front of the mirror until she could say them without looking at the script, and she could make all the right gestures without thinking.

Finally, she flopped on her bed and gave a big sigh. She lay there running her fingers through her short hair and thinking about what more she could do to prepare herself for the role of Julie. How could she make herself stand out?

She remembered reading about Robin Williams standing on his head during tryouts for the old TV show *Mork and Mindy*. It had gotten him the part, but standing on her head didn't seem like the right thing to do in this case. What could she do?

Suddenly, she got an idea and leapt from her bed. In the hallway she peaked over the railing and saw Brittany sitting in the foyer with the telephone stuck to the side of her head, as usual. Good, thought Beth, she'll be busy for at least another hour.

She checked Alicia's room and the door was closed. No light shone through the crack under it. Her little sister usually fell asleep as soon as her head hit the pillow.

Beth slipped down the hallway into Brittany's room and with one last peek behind her, closed the door quietly.

Tiptoeing to the closet, she searched through the hanging clothes. Way in the back was the blouse she was looking for. It was a soft pink taffeta that Brittany had had for a long time and didn't wear anymore. Putting it over her arm, Beth went to the bureau and opened the drawer where she knew Brittany kept her belts. The sequined dress belt that was wide in front was easy to find.

Back in her room, Beth slipped out of her sweat shirt and into the puff-sleeved blouse. Next she put on the dress belt and stood in front of her mirror. She still wasn't quite right.

She ran back to her closet and opened her trunk and threw the gorilla costume and other things on the floor until she found a blond wig. She ran her fingers through the long strands to straighten them and put it on. It looked perfect. Not bad, she thought, picking at the puff sleeves to make them stand up more.

Next she put her stage makeup on and went back to the full-length mirror to see herself. She pulled the hair over one shoulder and turned in a full circle so she could see from all angles.

A smile came across her face. The jeans she was wearing, the sequined belt, and the puff-sleeved blouse were a mixture of old and new. If she didn't look like a modern version of the pictures of what women wore in Shakespeare's day, no one would. And this was better than standing on her head on a couch. Look out tryouts. Here comes Beth Barry.

CHAPTER

*T*he next day at the tryouts, Beth stood behind the curtains and peeked out at the stage. She was wearing the pink taffeta blouse with the puffed sleeves and had the sequined belt and the wig in a brown paper bag that she gripped tightly behind her.

She had done her warm-up exercises until she thought she would hyperventilate. If she did any more stretches, her perspiration would gross out everybody, including Mr. Levine.

Most of the other kids were standing by themselves reading their parts or just looking worried. Mr. Levine was at the center of the stage talking to a tall, distinguished-looking man with a gray mustache and beard. He had to be Mr. Stapleton.

While Beth was watching, Taffy Sinclair went up to Mr. Levine and whispered something. He seemed interested and nodded as he wrote something on his clipboard. The nerve of her, thought Beth. She's just trying to be noticed by Mr. Stapleton.

"All right, everyone!" called Mr. Levine. "Gather round.

"You must all have guessed by now that this gentleman is Mr. Stapleton whom I told you about. He'll be helping me judge the tryouts.

"I've got one last-minute change in the list of candidates to mention to you. Taffy just told me that she won't be able to try out for the part of Julie. She and her parents have talked it over, and her schedule of modeling, acting lessons, and other professional commitments is just too much for her to be in our play. She's afraid she could be called away for an important job in Hollywood at any time and have to drop out." A murmur went through the crowd of kids. "It's our loss, Taffy," continued Mr. Levine, "but we understand. I want to thank you for telling me."

Beth couldn't believe it. Taffy was dropping out of the tryouts? She was the toughest competition for the part. Maybe I really do have a chance to win the role now, she thought.

"Let's start out with the role of Ronnie," Mr. Levine said, reading from his clipboard. "Then we'll do Julie, her mother, her father, and then Ronnie's mother and father. Garrett Boldt will be first, then Chet Miller, and last but not least, Billy Randall. Please take seats, and Garrett, if you would start at line five on page four and read through page fifteen, I'd appreciate it. I'll feed you Julie's lines."

Beth took a seat with the others to watch. Mr. Levine and Mr. Stapleton sat in the front row and made notes as Garrett, Chet, and Bill read their parts.

As each boy finished, and it got closer and closer to the girls' turns, Beth's hands got clammier and clammier. With Taffy out of the tryouts, she knew she should feel better, but she was still afraid she would goof her lines or her wig would fall off or something else dumb would happen. The kids applauded when the boys were finished. Beth thought all three had read very well.

"Okay!" Mr. Levine called. "Kaci Davis, Laura McCall, and Beth Barry, in that order. Would you please read Julie's part on those same pages? I'll read Ronnie's part."

Beth gulped and then climbed the stairs to the stage with her paper bag in her hand.

Standing in the wings by the curtains with Laura, Beth watched anxiously as Kaci read her part from the script and gestured dramatically as she moved around the stage. She's good, thought Beth, but she's moving around too much, and she's not staying in the light. She looked at Mr. Levine and Mr. Stapleton to see their reations. They were making notes and watching Kaci very carefully. When Kaci finished, the kids in the audience applauded.

When Mr. Levine called Laura's name, she gave Beth an icky-sweet smile and stepped out on the stage carrying her script. Beth crossed her eyes at her. Laura looked as if she knew she had the part already.

Beth's hands were sweating like miniature waterfalls. She wished she had half of Laura's confidence. She took the belt and wig from the bag and put them on. She wished she had a mirror to see how she looked. Was the wig on straight or was it crooked? She started taking deep breaths and read over the first few lines she was going to read.

"Beth Barry!" called Mr. Levine. She heard the kids clapping for Laura. Would they clap for her when she finished, or would there be total silence?

Beth dropped the script on the floor, smoothed her wig the best she could, pulled her shoulders back, and walked out onto the stage. She went directly to the front of the stage and raised her head just the way she had practiced. The lights glared in her eyes so that she couldn't see Mr. Levine and Mr.

Stapleton, but she smiled toward where she knew they were sitting.

She waited a moment for effect and heard some of the kids in the audience talking. Had her wig slipped? A chill of panic ran through her. Did she look funny? Were they laughing at her?

She froze and it seemed as if she would never be able to move again. The smile on her face felt stiff as she tried to remember the first line. She thought of the script lying on the floor in the wings where she had dropped it and wished she had it back.

Then she remembered her instructions and took a deep breath and thought about Julie, and the feeling of being her came back. Beth turned and walked away from the edge of the stage and turned again to face the lights, and the words from the script came tumbling back into her mind.

She tapped her foot loudly and then turned quickly as if the knocking had come from somewhere else. She reached out and opened an imaginary door.

"Ronnie! What are you doing here? You know my mom and dad will be furious."

When Beth had finished acting the part, she returned to the front of the stage, smiled, and bowed. She was stunned when she heard the applause, which was much louder than it had been for Kaci or

Laura. In the front row she could make out Mr. Levine and Mr. Stapleton applauding, too. A thrill ran through her until she was almost shaking, and a tear ran down each cheek. She felt like a star!

CHAPTER

7

"**I** did it! I did it! I did it!" squealed Beth, doing three quick cheerleading jumps. "I got the part!"

"We saw you!" Jana said, laughing, as she, Melanie, Christie, and Katie hopped around her. "We sneaked in to watch. You were *great*!"

"I can't get over the way you came on stage and just stood there smiling at everyone. You looked so cool," said Katie. "I think that's what wowed them."

"I liked the wig. It surprised everyone," added Christie.

"And the clothes. Don't forget the clothes," injected Jana. "You should have seen Mr. Levine's and

45

Mr. Stapleton's faces when you came onto the stage. They sat up in their seats right away."

"We're so proud of you," said Christie. She hugged Beth, and Beth hugged her back.

"You bet we are," said Katie.

Beth felt as if her grin stretched from one ear to the other. She was so happy.

"And boy are you lucky," said Christie. "Chet Miller's going to play the part of Ronnie."

"She's also lucky that Garrett didn't get the part," said Melanie. "I would have killed her and taken over the part of Julie for myself."

"I can't believe that Taffy dropped out," said Beth.

"I think you would have won with her in it, anyway," Melanie reassured her.

"I don't know," Beth said slowly. "It would have been a *lot* tougher."

"Well, you did it, and that's what counts," said Christie, hugging her again.

"Why don't we celebrate and go to the movies together tonight," suggested Jana. "We can wear our Fabulous Five T-shirts."

"Great idea!" responded Katie. "We'll show everybody The Fabulous Five are still sticking together."

"Right on!" shouted Melanie.

"Oh, I can't," said Christie. "Keith asked me if I'd go to the movies with him."

Beth felt as if she had just been run over by the whole Wakeman football team and maybe Miss Wolfe, too.

"It's okay with you, isn't it, Beth?" Christie asked. "I only gave him a tentative yes. I won't do it if you don't want me to."

Beth's face felt as if it had been starched stiff when she tried to smile. "Oh. Oh, no. That's okay. I said you could date him."

"Good," responded Christie, looking genuinely relieved. "I really didn't *think* you'd mind. Especially after you said you were going to break up with him anyway. But I just wanted to make sure. Actually it might make it easier for you to break up with him if I do go out with him."

"I hadn't thought of that," said Beth, putting on her best acting face.

Beth hopped out of the van and waved good-bye to her father. She felt good on the outside wearing her red T-shirt that said THE FABULOUS FIVE in gold letters, with her red socks and bright red earrings, but on the inside she was dreading running into Christie and Keith. How would they look together? What would she say? What would she do?

Katie, Jana, and Melanie were easy to spot in their red outfits, and she waved to them.

"Look at everyone watching us," said Melanie. "I bet we look super in our new Fabulous Five T-shirts."

"I feel as if I'm on display," said Jana. "It's like the time we took modeling lessons at Tanninger's Department Store and had to walk out on the stage in front of everybody."

"Look, there's Taffy with Cory Dillon," Katie said, pointing. Taffy was wearing a beautiful matching pink sweater-and-pants outfit with a flower pattern. She and Cory were headed their way.

"Well, look who's back into T-shirts," said Taffy. "Are you starting another club against someone?" Beth knew she was referring to the time when The Fabulous Five had had a club against her back in Mark Twain Elementary. It had served Taffy right then, but Taffy seemed a whole lot nicer since they'd come to Wakeman Junior High.

"Oh, by the way, Beth," Taffy added. "Congratulations on getting the lead part in the play."

"Thanks. I was surprised that you dropped out," answered Beth.

"I thought it over and realized my schedule is just *too* demanding for me to do the part, so I thought I'd let one of you have it," she said, putting her arm through Cory's possessively. "I've got all the success

I need." She tugged at Cory's arm and they walked off.

"She hasn't changed much, has she?" asked Katie.

"Not at all, if you ask me," said Beth. "She just has other things to do than bug us the way she did at Mark Twain Elementary."

"Here come Christie and Keith," said Jana. She looked quickly at Beth.

Beth struggled to keep her face looking happy as Christie waved and headed with Keith toward them.

"Hi," said Christie. Beth saw that Keith looked embarrassed.

"Hi," she answered cheerfully with the others. There was no way she was going to let Keith see that she was hurt because he was with Christie.

"Do you guys have your tickets yet?" Beth asked, smiling at them both.

"We got here early and have been talking to everybody," said Christie. "Randy and Scott are over there, and I saw Tony a little while ago. He and Clarence Marshall were arguing about something. I think it was because Tony was wearing an earring again.

"I feel like a traitor not being with you guys," Christie added. "But at least I'm wearing my Fabulous Five T-shirt."

The conversation seemed to go on forever. The

more they talked, the longer Beth had to look at Christie and Keith standing together as if they were boyfriend and girlfriend.

The knot in Beth's stomach grew larger and larger. Finally, Christie and Keith left to go into the theater. Beth held back the tears that were building up behind her eyes.

She pretended to be looking for the best seats as she led Katie, Jana, and Melanie down the aisle. She was actually looking as much for Christie and Keith as she was for a place to sit. She didn't want to be anywhere near them if she could help it.

Then she saw them. They were in the center a few rows in front of them.

"Here! Here are some good seats," she said, screeching to a halt so fast that Katie ran into her. She ducked into a row next to Clarence Marshall and Joel Murphy.

"What?" asked Melanie, looking at Clarence and Joel, who were grinning at them. The two boys each had two boxes of popcorn, which they obviously intended to throw after the lights went out. "Look, Beth. There are four empty seats over there. I think we can see better from there." Melanie turned, and Beth, Katie, and Jana followed her.

"You obviously didn't see Clarence and Joel," Jana whispered to Beth as they settled into the other seats.

Beth cringed. She would rather have sat next to Clarence and Joel than where they were now. They were just two rows behind Christie and Keith, and there was no way she could help but look at them during the movie.

Beth slouched down in her seat and concentrated on eating her popcorn one piece at a time.

CHAPTER

"*H*ow can you see the screen from way down there?" asked Jana as the movie started.

"Oh, I can see fine," answered Beth. "I'm looking between shoulders."

"Oh," said Jana, giving Beth an odd look.

From the deep hole she had made in her seat, Beth could watch the tops of the actors' heads as they walked back and forth across the screen. Who cares, she said angrily to herself, from what the actors are saying, this movie doesn't seem very interesting anyway. Maybe if I try, I can go to sleep and wake up after the movie's over and everyone's gone home.

Even slouched down the way she was, she could still see Christie's and Keith's heads close to each other. Keith said something to Christie and she laughed. Then Christie tried to put popcorn in his mouth and ended up stuffing his cheeks full. Keith ate the popcorn while Christie laughed at him again. Tears came to Beth's eyes. They were acting as if they had been going together a long time.

Beth tried not to look at them. She listened as hard as she could to what the actors were saying and looked around the theater at the decorations on the ceiling and the long drapes. She wondered what it cost them to have the drapes cleaned. How many rows there were, and how many seats were in each row. But before she knew it was happening, her treacherous eyes had returned to the black silhouettes of Christie's and Keith's heads.

Will he put his arm around her? I'll get up and walk out of here if he does *that*, Beth thought. Christie's leaning to talk to Keith now. Their heads are almost touching. What's she saying? Are they talking about me?

They're laughing again, Beth thought, squirming. She bent forward to try and hear but bumped her nose on the seat in front of her instead. Jana flashed her another look.

"Are you okay?" she whispered.

Beth nodded and rubbed her nose. She slumped

back down in the seat angrily. This time she held up the popcorn box as if she were trying to read what it said on the side. It blocked her view of Keith and Christie and the screen. But even without the box of popcorn, she wouldn't have been able to see the movie. She was looking at things through watery eyes.

Beth struggled to wake up the next morning. She had hardly slept the night before and had dreams of Christie and Keith walking hand in hand on a sandy beach lined with palm trees with sea gulls flying overhead. She pulled on her bathrobe and padded down the hall to the bathroom.

Yuk! she thought, looking at her red eyes. I might have to use my stage makeup today to get rid of these bags. I look like someone out of a vampire movie.

She paused, remembering the time she had gotten that terrible zit and had colored it over as if it were a bruise so Keith wouldn't see it. She giggled at the memory. She had put foundation over the bruise when she had gone to cheer at a game. Her perspiration made the foundation run, and the red bruise looked like blood and everyone thought she was bleeding to death. And I did it all so Keith wouldn't know I got zits, she thought.

The stadium was filling up quickly as Beth joined the other cheerleaders on the sidelines that afternoon. She looked out on the field where the teams were practicing and saw Keith, looking gorgeous in his red and gold uniform. She could swear that he looked in her direction a couple of times. Had he smiled at her? It looked as if he had.

"Okay, everybody!" Kaci Davis yelled through her megaphone. "Let's warm up with Out of Sight."

Beth took her position in the lineup as they began the cheer.

> "We're number one,
> and we can't be beat!
> We're coming on strong.
> Can you feel the heat?"

Beth saw Jana, Christie, and Katie climbing the stairway into the stands. She looked over her shoulder to see if Keith was looking at Christie and did a herkie when the rest of the team did a spread eagle. When the cheer was over, Kaci frowned at her.

At least I ought to get some credit for doing a herkie, thought Beth. It's a lot harder to do than a split anyway.

The team did two more cheers and Beth goofed one more time. "What's wrong?" Melanie asked her. "You missed two jumps."

"I just haven't gotten warmed up yet. I'll be all right."

Beth glanced at the players again. Keith was looking in her direction. He was looking at her, she just knew it.

"Yea, Keith!" came a shout from behind her, and Keith waved.

Beth spun and looked up into the stands. Christie was on her feet and waving both hands at Keith. Beth's heart sank and resentment washed over her. He hadn't been looking at Beth, after all. He had been watching for Christie.

Wakeman kicked off and Georgetown drove the ball eighty yards for a touchdown on their first possession. Beth counted four times that Mike Saharis carried the ball, and he gained a bunch of yards. If he kept that up, it would be tough for Keith to catch him no matter how well Keith did.

On the first play after the kickoff, Randy Kirwan handed the ball off to Keith, and he came thundering toward the sideline with three Georgetown players in pursuit. He cut downfield and was hit by a big player and sent sprawling. The ball came loose and a Georgetown player fell on it. Keith got up and Beth could see he was angry with himself for fumbling.

Wakeman held Georgetown to no gain for two plays, then Mike Saharis broke through the line and went forty yards for a touchdown.

The rest of the first half was a lot of the same. Every time Keith got the ball, he was hit at the line of scrimmage or dropped for a loss.

Beth watched him try time and time again to break through the line. She could tell by the look on his face that he was giving it everything he had, but it just wasn't good enough.

In the second half, the Wakeman team switched tactics, and Randy started throwing the ball. Shane Arrington caught a pass for a twenty-yard gain, and it took four Georgetown players to bring him down. Scott Daly caught another and made it into the end zone for a touchdown.

Melanie went wild and threw her pom-pons into the air. Two of the boys that Melanie liked were making big plays, and she couldn't decide which one to yell for the loudest.

On the extra point try, Randy gave the ball to Keith, and he was almost destroyed at the line of scrimmage. Beth's heart broke when she saw him crawl out from under the pileup and limp off the field. His red and gold uniform was dirty and grass-stained, and his face was beet red from the effort he had given.

The final score was Georgetown twenty-one and Wakeman twenty. It was Wakeman's first loss of the season. Worst yet, Beth knew that Mike Saharis had gained about a zillion yards and Keith hadn't gained any. He wouldn't beat out Mike to be first in the league in yards gained.

As the teams trotted off the field, Keith walked behind with his head down. For a second Beth wanted to run up to him and hug him and tell him that it was okay that he hadn't gained a bunch of yards.

But just as she started to move toward him, Christie came onto the field and ran to him. Beth stopped short and turned away.

CHAPTER

*T*he crowd at Bumpers was subdued when Beth and Melanie got there. Beth could tell by the way everyone was talking quietly that they were taking Wakeman's first loss hard.

"There they are," said Melanie, waving to Jana, Christie, and Katie. Their friends motioned them over to the big corner booth that had lots of space for kids to sit.

"Boy, what a game," said Jana with disgust.

"We lost by one measly point," growled Christie.

"Well it wasn't Keith's fault! He tried to make that extra point!" snapped Beth. "He did the best he could."

"Whoa," said Katie.

Christie looked at Beth with her mouth opened in surprise. "No one said it was Keith's fault. He wasn't the only player on the field."

"We know Keith did his best," said Jana.

"I just mean, he had a bad day. Everyone has a bad day now and then."

Beth took a deep breath. Why had she jumped on Christie that way?

She changed the subject quickly. "Randy and Shane really did well. How many passes did Randy complete?"

Jana's face took on a glow of pride. "Ten, I think."

The conversation about the game continued, and Beth tried to say as little as possible as she listened to her friends. She had just let her emotions get the best of her, and she didn't want it to happen again.

But each time Christie said something about Keith, Beth had to bite her lip to keep from saying something nasty. Christie was talking about Keith as if *she* were the one who had been going with him since way back in Mark Twain Elementary.

When the players arrived, they came in without their usual waving of arms and shouts of triumph. Randy and Scott walked over to the booth where The Fabulous Five were sitting, and Keith and Shane went to the counter to get sodas.

"I need to get something to drink," Beth said, trying to sound casual. "Can I get anyone else anything?" She took orders and got in line behind Keith.

At first he didn't notice her. Beth stood close to him and tried to make it appear that she wasn't aware of whom she was standing next to, either. She thought about bumping into him accidentally, but that seemed too obvious.

Finally, Shane noticed her. "Hi, Beth."

Keith turned around quickly. "Hi." He smiled sheepishly and shuffled his feet.

"Oh, hi," Beth said as if she had just seen him, too. "I didn't know you were standing there," she fibbed. "I gave a few cheers for you today."

"I guess they didn't work too well," he answered. "I pretty well blew it. I couldn't even score the extra point that would have tied the game. And Mike Saharis must have gotten a hundred yards."

Beth didn't know what to say. He looked as if he were blaming Wakeman's loss on himself. She wished she could say something that would make him feel better.

"You couldn't do it all yourself," she said. It was Christie who had said Keith wasn't the only Wakeman player on the field, but she wasn't going to tell him that.

"Thanks," he said, and he looked as if he really meant it.

"Beth?" His voice sounded serious.

"Yes?" she answered, leaning toward him.

His eyes softened, and he opened his mouth to speak. He hesitated, and Beth felt as if she were going to melt down into her shoes. He was going to say something important, she just knew it. Maybe he was going to apologize about dating Christie and say he wanted everything to be the way it had been before.

"I decided I wanted a soda, too."

Beth whipped her head around at the sound of Christie's voice behind her.

"Hi, Keith," Christie said cheerfully, breaking the mood.

Disappointment washed over Beth like a tidal wave. Why did Christie have to barge in just at that moment? Now Beth would never know what Keith was going to say.

The rest of the afternoon passed by in a blur for Beth. She got the sodas, and Keith squeezed into the booth between her and Christie. She thought about leaving but somehow couldn't pull herself away. She kept hoping that she would have another chance to talk with Keith and find out what he had been about to say.

Keith was quiet as the others talked, and she wished she could read his mind. Was he thinking about what he had been about to say when Christie interrupted him? Or was he thinking about the football game?

She looked at him out of the corners of her eyes. He was watching Christie as she told a funny story. Is she showing off for Keith? Beth wondered.

For the first time since she had known Christie, Beth felt as if she couldn't trust her. Was she trying to steal Beth's boyfriend? Right in front of everyone?

"I've got to go home," said Jana. "It's getting late."

"Me, too," said Katie. Everyone else said they had to leave, too.

Beth watched Keith closely, hoping he would walk her home instead of Christie. He left with Scott instead.

Disappointed, Beth pulled on her jacket and headed for the door.

"Oh, Beth!" Christie called to her once they were outside. "I need to ask you something."

Beth waited as she caught up with her.

"I wanted to ask you what kind of music and pizza Keith likes. He's coming over tonight to listen to records and I wanted to be prepared."

Beth looked at Christie in astonishment. *How could she ask Beth about Keith's favorite music and pizza?* It was bad enough stealing him from her, but now she had the nerve to ask her something like that.

Beth gave Christie an angry look and turned and ran.

"Beth!" she heard Christie call after her. "What's wrong?"

Beth didn't stop running until she reached home.

CHAPTER

10

"*B*eth! Telephone!" Brittany yelled up the stairway.

Beth struggled to get up from her bed, where she had been lying since she had gotten home. She rubbed the dampness from her eyes.

Was it Keith calling to ask if he could come over tonight? Maybe he had realized after seeing her today that he would rather be with her than Christie. Of course he wouldn't be able to tell Christie why he had broken his date with her. Beth would keep it a secret.

It was Christie instead.

"Beth, I'm just calling to see if you're all right.

You're not sick or something, are you? The way you ran off this afternoon scared me."

Beth took a deep breath. She couldn't let Christie know how she really felt. She had her pride, and they had been friends for a long time. She couldn't let Christie know she was angry at her, especially not after she had told Christie that it was okay for her to go out with Keith.

"No. Everything's okay," Beth lied. "I just remembered that I had to get home, that's all."

"Oh. Well, you looked mad at me, and I was trying to figure out what I could have done."

"Mad at you?" Beth asked, pretending to be surprised. Christie really didn't understand. "No. I'm not mad at you," she continued in her best stage voice.

"Good," Christie said happily. "We've been friends for a long time, and we've always told each other when something's wrong. I don't want that to change."

"Everything's okay," Beth lied. "What did you want to ask me before?"

I wanted to find out what kind of records and pizza Keith likes. You know him better than I do."

"He likes sausage pizza," Beth said. Then she recited the records that they usually listened to when he came over. She thought she would die with each and every title she named. They all had special meaning to her and brought back memories of their sitting together holding hands.

Beth slowly put the phone back in its cradle after Christie had hung up. Christie seemed to have been truly worried that Beth might be mad at her. She really doesn't know how I feel, Beth thought, putting her hands on her cheeks. She's too honest to act as if she didn't when she did.

Back in her room, Beth got out her picture album. There were lots of pictures of her family and her in the first few pages. They were mostly taken when she was little.

Then she came to the pictures that were taken at Mark Twain Elementary. She giggled in spite of herself. Jana, Melanie, Katie, and Christie looked so young in the pictures. She did, too.

Next she found the pictures that they had exchanged when they left Mark Twain Elementary last year. Christie looked so pretty. Her blond hair was always neatly brushed, and she had a fresh-scrubbed, all-American look. And she always seemed to know what she was doing and what was right. Not like me, Beth thought, who's always getting into trouble.

Keith's picture made him look so handsome with his sandy blond hair and blue eyes. She took it out of the album and looked at what he had written on the back.

> *To Beth,*
> *Your boyfriend, Keith*

A tear trickled down her cheek. That was the first time he had ever called himself her boyfriend. She would remember it the rest of her life, just like the first time he had kissed her.

She put the picture next to her own and looked at them. Next she put his picture next to Christie's. Would people start thinking of Keith and Christie as a couple rather than Keith and Beth? Keith and Beth sounded so much better. She said the words out loud.

Sometimes she felt mad at Christie, and sometimes she didn't. It was so confusing. After all, she had told Christie she wanted to break up with Keith. But why did Christie have to believe her so easily? Was Christie waiting for the opportunity to date Keith?

No! Christie was one of her very *best* friends. She was only dating Keith because Beth had said it was okay. Beth felt guilty about all the bad things she had felt about Christie. But couldn't Christie see that it really wasn't okay?

And what about Keith? Was he really so angry

over the play that he didn't want to date her anymore? Or was she such a great actress that she had
convinced him he wasn't as important as the play?

One more time, she thought. One more time my
big mouth has gotten me into trouble, and this may
be the worst time of all. I can't possibly go to school
and Bumpers and other places and act as if I don't
care that one of my best friends is dating the boy I
care about. Beth settled back down on the bed with
the picture of Keith in her hand. Staring at it with
tears falling from her eyes, she wished there were a
way to take back the angry words she had said to
him earlier that week.

Her friends were at The Fabulous Five's spot by the
fence Monday morning as Beth arrived at school.
Jana, Katie, and Melanie were laughing as they listened to something Christie was telling them. Beth
screwed up her courage as she approached them.

"Hi," she said as cheerfully as she could manage.

"Oh, Beth," said Christie. "I've got to tell you
how funny it was when I had all of Keith's favorite
records out when he came over. He couldn't imagine
how he and I liked exactly the same music. And
when I told him my favorite pizza was sausage, you
should have seen his eyes light up." She was laughing so hard she was doubled over. "Thanks for helping me," she said between giggles.

"That's okay," Beth responded, trying to keep her voice up.

"And do you know what else we did?" Christie asked the group as she started laughing again.

"I just remembered. I've got to study for social studies," said Beth, breaking away and heading for the school. She was running by the time she reached the door.

She pushed her way inside and bumped into Mona Vaughn.

"Excuse me!" she said, and headed for the nearest girl's room. There were three girls inside, but they were busy combing their hair and didn't notice her as she went into one of the stalls.

Beth sat down and covered her face with her hands and the tears ran through her fingers. She shook with silent sobs, and visions of Keith and Christie having fun in Christie's family room filled her mind.

How was she ever going to make it through the day?

CHAPTER

11

*B*eth saw Christie and Keith walking in the halls holding hands four times that morning. Once she even had to duck into a classroom so she wouldn't have to confront them. "Oops! Excuse me," said Beth as she stepped back into the hall and ran ino Heather Clark and Sara Sawyer.

"Heather and I were just talking about you," said Sara.

"Oh?" Her curiosity aroused, Beth fell in step with them.

"Well, about you and Christie really," said Heather. "You guys are really cool, the way Christie quit going with Jon Smith and now she's dating Keith, and it doesn't even seem to bother you."

"How do you do it?" asked Sara. "I'd be so jealous."

Beth shrugged her shoulders, suddenly wishing she were somewhere else. She couldn't let them know she was just acting as if Christie and Keith's dating didn't bother her. It was the hardest acting job she had ever done, and she didn't even want the part.

"I bet they had it planned all along," Heather said to Sara.

"That's it!" she said turning back to Beth. "You did, didn't you? I bet you're going to date Jon and Christie is going to date Keith. Gosh, you guys are cool."

"No, I'm not going to date Jon," answered Beth. "I haven't even seen Jon for a while."

"Oh." Heather seemed deflated that she hadn't guessed right. "Well, I still think you guys are cool. I couldn't stand it if my best friend dated the guy I had been going with. I mean, even if I didn't like him anymore. It would seem as if my privacy had been invaded or something."

Beth made a quick right at an intersection in the hallway and left them standing looking after her.

If she hadn't felt so bad, she would have laughed

at what Heather and Sara had said. They thought she was cool, that she didn't care that Christie and Keith were dating. What a joke! she thought. It just proves how good an actress I really am.

Beth took longer than usual in the girls' room washing her hands for lunch. She wanted to miss the rush of kids entering the cafeteria right at noon. She wasn't sure she could have another conversation like the one with Heather and Sara without crying. She would die if she broke down in front of people.

She took a deep breath and forced a smile as she entered the cafeteria. No one seemed to notice her as she picked up a tray and utensils. She hung back to leave space between herself and Curtis Trowbridge and Whitney Larkin so she wouldn't have to talk to them. She didn't want to take any chances on someone's starting a conversation about Keith and Christie and how *cool* she was for not caring. She'd probably break down and start blubbering right there in front of the whole cafeteria.

Jana, Katie, Christie, and Melanie were sitting at The Fabulous Five's regular table when she came through the line. They scooted over to make room for her.

"Hi, Julie," said Melanie.

Beth smiled and said, "Hi."

"Is Tony going before the Teen Court this week?" Christie asked Katie.

Katie blushed. "No, not this week. At least not that I know of."

"Give him a chance. He'll think of a way to get there," said Jana.

"Hey, look," Katie protested. "Tony's not bad. He's just misunderstood. He helped organize the march for the hungry, didn't he?"

"We know he did," said Jana. "We were just teasing you."

"I wonder if he would have done it if Katie hadn't been his partner." Melanie kidded.

"Did you all see how everyone looked at us Friday night when we were wearing our T-shirts?" asked Katie. "I think they went over really big."

"I'll say," said Christie. "Melinda Thaler came up to me today and told me how great she thought we looked."

"Maybe we ought to go to the movie together again this Friday night and wear them then," suggested Katie.

"I already told Randy I'd go with him," said Jana.

"And I'm going with Scott," said Melanie.

"Oh, I didn't think before I suggested it," said Katie. "Tony asked me to go with him, too. I guess that shoots that idea."

"It was a good idea," said Christie. "Maybe we should pick one day out of the week and wear our T-shirts to school." They all agreed.

Christie looked at Beth as the others went on talking. "Do you have a date for the movies on Friday?" she asked, a look of concern on her face.

The question caught Beth by surprise, and she shook her head no. She was afraid to speak because her voice might quiver.

"If you don't get a date, why don't you go with Keith and me?" Christie asked. "You know Keith won't mind, and I hate to see you not go."

Beth braced herself before she answered. She knew that Christie was trying to be nice, but how could she go with her and Keith? It would be like sticking a knife in her own heart.

She fought to keep the smile on her face and the tears out of her eyes. She remembered one of the rules of acting: concentrate on your lines. That's exactly what she did.

"Maybe," she answered smiling. "I might still get a date before then, though."

It's like a part in a play, she told herself. If I decide that this character, named Beth, is not in love with this other character named Keith Masterson, and it doesn't bother her to talk about him, I can do it. I can do it if I can just remember I'm acting a part in a play.

CHAPTER

12

"All right, everyone," said Mr. Levine. "Let's call it a day. You all did very well. Remember, we're doing the scene next where Ronnie's parents come to Julie's house. Beth, may I speak to you a minute?"

Beth gathered her books from the chair and followed him off the stage. She knew she had blown a couple of her lines, but she was tired and had lost her concentration. And with Keith and Christie on her mind, she had had a terrible time remembering to be Julie. She hoped she hadn't done so badly that he would chew her out. She didn't realize that acting could be such hard work.

"I've got to tell you, Beth, that you're doing a fine

job. I'm amazed that you've learned your lines so quickly, and you seem to understand the part of Julie very well. I normally wouldn't expect someone in the seventh grade to do as well as you are."

His words were wonderful to hear. They were the best thing that had happened to her in the last several days.

"Do you really mean it?" she asked, afraid he would say no, that he was just kidding.

"I certainly do. You remember Mr. Stapleton who was here last week at the tryouts, don't you?" he asked.

"Yes."

"Well, there's a strong possibility that he'll be coming back for our opening night. I'd like for him to see you after we've had a chance to practice. He might have some suggestions for you."

Beth felt as if she were floating on air as she left the auditorium. Mr. Levine had said she was a *good* actress. He hadn't said great, but that would come if she worked hard enough.

She had always felt she could be an actress, but Mr. Levine's compliment made it seem much more real. It was like getting a stamp of approval. Like making an A on a test you thought you had failed. It was even better than having your friends and family tell you how good you were. They nearly always told you that, even if they didn't mean it a whole lot.

Beth put her books away after she had finished studying that night. She had worked particularly hard on social studies to make up for not having studied as hard as she should have before the test.

She picked up her script and opened it to the scene they would be working on Wednesday. It was kind of ironic. Now that she had the role of Julie, she still had to study the script, but it didn't seem as hard. She had more time than she had thought she would have.

I don't really have so much to do that I couldn't study with Keith sometimes, she thought. But it doesn't look as if that makes much difference now. If she had only known when they were talking about it before.

She hadn't talked to him since she saw him in line at Bumpers. He could have called, but he hadn't.

Beth fell onto the bed and thumbed through the script. It was sad that the one thing she had always wanted to do was costing her the boy she liked best.

Would it have made a difference if she had told Keith she wouldn't go out for the play? She had thought about it before, and she wondered again if he had just been looking for an excuse to break up with her.

Keith had been complaining to her about not having enough time together ever since Christie broke up with Jon. Had Keith wanted to date Christie all along?

She thought back to their days at Mark Twain Elementary and tried to remember any clues she might have missed. Were there times when Keith seemed to hang around Christie a lot? She couldn't remember any, but that didn't mean there hadn't been.

She sighed. Keith obviously liked Christie or he wouldn't be dating her and spending so much time with her at school. Did he think she was prettier than Beth? She is smarter. There's no doubt about that. But I'm no dummy, she thought angrily. She rubbed the moisture from her eyes with the corner of her pillow slip.

It was getting harder and harder to talk to Christie. It seemed as if all she ever wanted to talk about anymore was Keith and what music he liked and what pizza he liked and how much fun he was. I can't talk about him all the time. It hurts too much.

Deep down Christie must know how much Beth still liked him. How could she not? Why couldn't she see that her going with Keith was tearing up Beth?

Because I'm such a good actress, thought Beth. I told her it would be all right if she dated Keith. *I* told her I was thinking of breaking up with him the way she had with Jon. But why did she have to believe me?

Beth took her time getting ready for school the

next morning. She changed clothes three times trying to decide what to wear and actually managed to eat breakfast, even though Alicia was talking the entire time and Agatha was begging for the empty cereal bowl to lick.

She slowed her pace as she neared the school grounds and timed her entrance perfectly. The school bell was ringing just as she turned onto the walk that led to the door. She waved at her friends, who were standing at their regular place, and went on into the building. It would be easier if she didn't have to talk to them.

During the day, Beth walked through the hallways as quickly as she could between each of her classes and pretended to study as soon as she got into the classrooms. Between her second and third class, she caught a glimpse of Keith and Christie talking in the hall, and she turned and went the other way.

When lunch period came, Beth took the sandwich she had brought from home and went out onto the school grounds with her script. She found an isolated spot in the sun at the side of the building and made herself comfortable.

Beth read through her part and ate her lunch, then she read it again. By the time the bell rang ending the lunch period, she had read through it so many times she thought she could say it backwards.

"Where have you been?" asked Jana. She and Katie had caught up with her in the hall. "We missed you at lunch."

"I was studying my part," Beth responded, holding up the script. "I thought it would be easier if I brought my lunch today and went outside to read."

"How's it going?" Katie asked.

"You wouldn't believe it. Mr. Levine said he really liked what I was doing, and Mr. Stapleton might be here for opening night. Mr. Levine said he wants him to see me act. Can you imagine how I'd feel if he offered to cast me in a part in a Broadway play? I get stage fright just thinking about it."

"Great!" said Jana.

"I guess not going with Keith has given you more time to study for your role," said Katie. "I like the way you've set your priorities and stuck with it. More girls ought to be like you."

"I agree," said Jana. "Only I don't think I could give up Randy the way you gave up Keith. And it's amazing how it doesn't even seem to bother you that he's dating Christie."

Beth felt her stomach tighten. Everyone thought she was doing such a great thing, and it was really just a mistake. If she hadn't opened her mouth and said all those dumb things to get even with Keith, she would still be going with him.

Beth shook her head and smiled in response to

Jana's comment. She couldn't make herself say anything.

"You really are in control of your life," said Katie. "Because of some of the, uh, excuse me . . . not so smart things you've done, I wouldn't have thought you could give up Keith for a career in acting."

Beth felt like an idiot standing in front of two of her best friends listening to them praise her for something she wished had never happened. It took real control for her not to break down and cry right then and there.

CHAPTER

13

Beth put her pom-pons on the pile with the others and walked onto the track leading to the stadium exit. Melanie was walking ahead of her with Scott, and they were laughing. Cory Dillon had his arm around Taffy, and several other girls were walking with boys.

Beth felt lonely. She and Keith had been going together so long, and he had always been there to make things more fun, more exciting for her. She felt there was a gigantic void in her life. Was this the way people felt when they got divorced? If it was, she didn't want to have anything to do with it. She walked with her head down, scuffing her shoes in the track surface.

"Hi." Keith's voice made her turn quickly. She tried to recover her composure and look as if she weren't as surprised as she really was. He was smiling down at her in that special way she thought he had reserved for her. Did he smile that way at Christie, too?

"Oh, hi," she said as casually as she could. Had her voice cracked? Had it quivered? She would die if it had.

"How's the play going?" Keith asked.

"Fine."

What else could she say? Should she tell him what Mr. Levine had said about how well she was doing, that he wanted Mr. Stapleton to see her act? No. The play was the thing that had come between them in the first place.

She changed the subject instead. "How's football going? Are you ready for the game with Jefferson this Saturday?"

"I think so." Then his face brightened. "Coach said I've still got a chance for the rushing title, after all. He said Georgetown has played one more game than we have, so I'm not as far behind Mike Saharis as I thought I was. I might be able to take him this Saturday."

Beth looked at his face beaming with excitement. He loved playing football so much. He always got excited when he talked about it. He told her how he dreamed of making the high school team and then going to college on a football scholarship. It had gotten so she wanted it for him almost as much as he did.

"I'll be cheering for you," she said, touching his arm.

"I know you will," he said softly. He opened his mouth again as if he wanted to say something more.

She felt herself getting weaker as she looked into his eyes. They were so intense. For a second she thought she saw tears in his eyes. Hold on, she told herself. Don't make a fool out of yourself.

"Uh," he seemed to search for something else to say. "Are you going to the movies Friday? Christie said she asked you to go with us."

Beth's world came crumbling down around her. She could have sworn that he was going to say something different, something more meaningful. He had just casually mentioned that Christie had told him they were going to the movies together as if it were nothing for him to have her along when he was holding hands with Christie. She felt like crying one more time.

Instead, she pulled up all her courage. This is just like a play, she reminded herself. I can do it! I can act as if nothing is wrong.

"I've got a date," she fibbed. And then before he

could ask her whom she was going with, she changed the subject.

"I've been wanting to see this movie," she said with a cheerful laugh. "I hear it's funnier than *Who Framed Roger Rabbit*."

Keith looked at her, and his eyes looked sad for a moment, and then he laughed, too. They stood there laughing together, but Beth wasn't laughing on the inside.

Beth followed Melanie into Bumpers. She had told Melanie that she had to get home to study, but Melanie had insisted she come, at least for one soda.

Christie and Jana were sitting in one of the bright red bumper cars, talking. When they saw Beth and Melanie, they all moved to a booth by the old Wurlitzer jukebox.

"Where's Katie?" asked Melanie.

"Teen Court," said Christie.

"I wonder if Tony's in trouble again?" Jana mused. "I thought it was funny the way she was telling you about how she liked the way you had set your priorities, Beth. You know, choosing a career in acting over going with Keith. Especially the way she's fallen for Tony."

"That is a riot," said Melanie. "And she's the one who's always on my case for liking boys."

"Beth and Christie are the ones who have it under control," Jana said admiringly. "Christie decided she would rather just be best friends with Jon, and Beth decided she didn't have time to go steady, and they both did it."

Beth listened to them talking. It was as if she were watching them on a television. It all didn't seem real. She just smiled and didn't say a word.

"When you put it that way, I guess we are a little special, eh, Beth?" Christie said, laughing and patting Beth's hand. "Leave it to us to start a new trend at Wacko. Women freed of male dominance. We ought to talk to Curtis Trowbridge about doing an article on us. Katie would love it. She might even write the article herself."

"Keith told me you have a date for the movies," said Christie. "Who's it with?"

"You'll have to wait and see," Beth said, crossing her fingers. Why had she told Keith she had a date when she didn't? Her big mouth was getting her in deeper and deeper again.

"You're not going to tell us?" asked Melanie. "No fair! I tell you everything about the boys I like."

"And everyone else who'll listen," said Christie.

"Are you all right, Beth?" Jana asked. "Your eyes look kind of funny."

"Sure," Beth responded, gripping her hands tightly under the table. "I'll be back in a minute."

She got up quickly and headed for the door marked
LADIES.

"We know where you're going," teased Melanie.

"Next time don't wait so long," Beth heard Christie say as the door closed behind her.

Beth ran into the nearest stall and put her head
against the wall. The cold metal pressed against her
forehead and her shoulders shook with sobs.

It wasn't funny. Why didn't her best friends understand? Couldn't they tell she was hurting inside?
She missed Keith something terrible, and there
wasn't anything she could do about getting him
back. And now she had told them she had a date
with someone else for the movies.

What could she do? If she told everyone the truth,
they would just feel sorry for her, and she didn't
want their pity. It wouldn't help get Keith back.
And Christie thought it was *so* funny. Maybe it was
easy for her to give up Jon. Maybe she hadn't cared
that much about him in the first place. But Beth had
never really wanted to give up Keith. What could
she do? Beth heard the door to the ladies' room
open, and she took a deep breath to stop her crying.

"Beth. Are you all right?" It was Jana.

"Of course," she answered through the partition.

"Are you sure? Is there anything I can do? You
looked as if you were going to cry."

"Cry?" Beth faked a laugh. "That's funny. Why

would I be crying?" she said, making her voice sound happy.

There was a moment of silence before Jana said, "Okay. You just didn't look right to me." Beth heard the door open and close.

She pulled herself together and peeked through a crack in the stall door. Jana was gone.

She came out quickly, ran cold water in the lavatory, and splashed it onto her face. Then she waited a few minutes while the red when out of her eyes.

When she returned to the booth, they were chattering about boys again. Jana gave Beth a quick look and went on talking.

"Did you hear?" asked Christie. "Keith was telling me that Georgetown has played one more game than Wacko. That means he still has a chance to beat that guy from Georgetown."

"Is that right?" asked Jana.

"Yes, and he's really excited about it. I told him, if he did really well I'd give him a big hug."

Beth felt as if she were going to explode. She was going to have to leave or break down in front of them.

"You know, Beth," Christie said. "I understand why you went with Keith so long. He's neat. You really know how to pick them."

CHAPTER

"Ronnie, your parents are here," whispered Chet Miller.

Beth flashed him a grateful look for the cue.

"Ronnie, your parents are here. You've got to stay hidden or they'll find you," she spoke the lines.

"Okay, cut," called Mr. Levine. "Beth, you need to sound more excited. Remember, you're afraid. If Ronnie's parents catch him in the closet, you know you'll never get to date him again. Put yourself in Julie's place. What if you were about to lose the boy you love? You'd be upset wouldn't you?"

"Yes, Mr. Levine."

It was the fifth time he had stopped the rehearsal

to give her instructions, and she had forgotten her lines three times. Chet had helped her get started again. He was awfully nice for a ninth-grader.

She knew her lines. She was sure she did. She had studied them over and over until she could say them in her sleep. The trouble was, when someone else was speaking their lines, Beth would start thinking about Keith. Then she wouldn't know where they were at in the script when it was her turn to speak again. It was embarrassing.

"Look, everyone," continued Mr. Levine, speaking to the group of actors on the stage. "We've got a little over a week to learn our parts. We were doing so well for a while, and now we seem to have hit a rough spot." Beth knew she was the rough spot he was talking about.

"So, let's call it quits for today. Now I want you to go over your lines really carefully tonight and tomorrow so we can have a great rehearsal on Friday. I'll see you then.

"Beth, can I talk to you a moment?" he asked.

Beth cringed. She knew she deserved it if he chewed her out for goofing up.

"I know you're trying hard, Beth. Maybe you're trying too hard. I suppose I shouldn't have told you about Mr. Stapleton's being here on opening night. Would it be better if I called him and asked him not to come?"

"No, I don't think so," she whispered. "I don't think I'm bothered about his being there. I'll try harder, honest I will."

He looked at her with a wry smile. "I'm sure you will," he said. "Just relax, and remember, it's just a part in a play. There will be lots more, and it can be fun if you let it."

Beth skipped going to Bumpers after rehearsal. She told herself that she had to practice and couldn't spare the time.

At the dinner table she was glad for once that she belonged to such a big family. Brian and Brittany argued over who should get to use the van on Friday and Saturday, her father bawled out Todd for acting up in school again, and Alicia talked as loud as she could just to attract attention. All the while, Agatha walked from chair to chair hoping for a handout. Everyone pretty much ignored Beth, and she didn't have to talk. She could just poke at her food and stay lost in her thoughts.

In her room that evening, Beth sat with the play script on her lap. What had started out being a lot of fun was beginning to turn into a drag. She had done so well at the tryouts and at the first rehearsal, and now all of a sudden she couldn't seem to concentrate.

She flipped open the script to the lines she hadn't been able to remember today.

Ronnie, your parents are here. You've got to stay hidden or they'll find you.

Why couldn't she have remembered them today? It was so embarrassing to have Mr. Levine stop the rehearsal to correct her. I wonder if he'll kick me out of the cast? Beth thought. I bet he wishes he had chosen Kaci. Even Laura McCall could do as well as me. There's still enough time for him to let one of them do the part.

She walked over to the bed and picked up the panda bear she had used in the parent project at school. It was chewed up where Agatha had gotten hold of it. She held it close and nuzzled her face into its neck.

Everything was so different at Wakeman Junior High. It wasn't at all like Mark Twain Elementary. When The Fabulous Five were sixth-graders, Jana went with Randy, Scott went with Melanie, and Keith went with her. There were no complications.

Beth had been in all the school plays and there hadn't been any problems. In fact Keith had played a part in one of them. He had been a robber and wore a flat cap with a bill and had a mustache painted on. They had laughed lots over how funny he looked.

She kissed the panda on the nose and sat down on the bed.

"And now he's mad because I'm in a play and have

to practice," she said to the bear. "It's not really fair. He practices football every day after school, and I don't say anything about it. In fact I'm happy for him, he likes it so much. I'm the one who should be mad." She sat the bear in her lap and held out its legs.

"Do you think it would make a difference to him if I dropped out of the play?" she asked it. "Mr. Levine could get either Kaci or Laura to take my place. They both know the part. But how could I tell Keith? And if I did, would he really want me back?"

She sighed, gazing out the window. "He should be happy for me that I got the role. But he's not. And I miss him so much."

CHAPTER

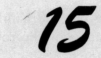

"Vell, Miss Beth Barry. Vould you like to join us in doing the next cheer? Or is it asking too much?" Miss Wolfe's German accent broke into Beth's daydream.

"Oh, I'm sorry." Beth jumped back into the lineup. She had been watching Keith and hadn't heard Miss Wolfe call an end to the break.

"What cheer is it?" Beth whispered frantically to Melanie.

"Count Down," Melanie whispered back.

Beth spread her feet apart and put her hands on her waist in the starting position.

"Count down ready!
Count down now!
Count down ready!
We'll show you how!"

Beth concentrated and jumped in perfect unison with the team.

"10-9-8-7-6-5-4-3-2-1!
Count down ready!
Let's run Warriors!
We're number one!"

"Very good, girls. Ve ver all together for a change." Miss Wolfe gave Beth an approving smile.

Beth sneaked another look at the football team. Keith had the ball and was running with one player on his back and another hanging on to his leg. They finally wrestled him to the ground, and the rest of the team applauded his effort.

Every time she looked he had tacklers all over him and was fighting to stay on his feet. Keith was trying terribly hard and was beginning to look exhausted. She hoped he wouldn't get hurt. The game with Jefferson was important to him and to Wakeman, but not that important. If he didn't get noticed by the high school coach it wouldn't be the end of the world.

"Okay, now ve vill do Electrify," ordered Miss Wolfe. Beth jumped into the starting position.

*   *   *

"Are you going to Bumpers?" Melanie asked Beth after practice was over.

"Oh, I don't know. I've got a lot of studying to do tonight, and I missed some of my lines at play rehearsal yesterday," said Beth. "I'd better go home and study."

"Study? Aren't you going a little overboard?" asked Melanie. "You brought your lunch and studied by yourself again today. You've never had trouble remembering your lines before."

"I know, but for some reason I'm having trouble this time."

"Oh, come on and go to Bumpers, Beth. It seems like we never see you anymore."

"You're beginning to sound like Keith." Beth was sorry she said it the way she did. She could tell by Melanie's face that she had hurt her feelings.

"Oh, I'm sorry, Melanie. I didn't mean to say it that way. All right, I'll go. But I can't stay long."

"There are Katie and Jana." Melanie grabbed Beth's arm and pulled her toward the booth where they were saving seats for them. Katie leaned across and whispered something to Jana.

"Here are the prides of the cheerleading squad," said Katie cheerfully, smiling up at Beth and Melanie.

"How are the prides of the Teen Court and *The Wigwam* yearbook?" asked Melanie, laughing.

Beth thought they all seemed extremely happy.

"You're still not going to tell us who you're going to the movies with?" asked Jana.

"Nope," said Beth, trying to sound self-assured and looking around.

"Where's Christie?" she asked, hoping she hadn't already guessed.

"She went to see Keith after practice," said Jana. "She'll be here later."

They talked about the usual things for a while, but Beth caught Jana and Katie looking at her oddly a couple of times. She sensed a stiffness to the conversation and tried to join in in spite of wishing she could leave before Christie and Keith got there.

"Beth," Jana said suddenly. "Are you mad at us?"

Beth was stunned by the question. "Why no, of course not," she answered wide-eyed. "Why would you think that?"

"Well, it seems like you've been avoiding us," said Katie. "And we thought we had done something to make you angry."

Beth laughed. She had been so involved in her own problems she hadn't thought about what her friends might be thinking about her not spending time with them.

"No, believe me, I'm not mad at you guys. I've just had a lot of things to think about."

"Good!" said Katie. "We were starting to worry. We thought you were avoiding us in the morning before school, and then during the lunch period you've started going outside by yourself. We didn't know what was wrong."

"And I could have sworn you were crying the other day when you went to the girls' room," said Jana. "You were almost running."

Beth smiled at her. "Being a member of The Fabulous Five is very important to me. You guys are my best friends."

"Whew! That's a relief," said Melanie. The conversation perked up considerably after that.

Beth looked at her friends. They *were* very important to her. She hated that it was Christie who was dating Keith. If it were anyone besides one of The Fabulous Five, she could throw a tantrum and fight for him. But if she got into a fight with Christie, it would probably break up the group. She would never want to be the one who caused that.

She should have known that they would suspect something was wrong. They had been her friends almost forever and had come to her rescue lots of times. Like the time she had gone back to Mark Twain Elementary to hide when she thought she was the cause of her mother's being ill. They had even gotten a search party together to find her.

How much longer can I keep how I feel a secret? she asked herself. What will happen if Christie finds out I still like Keith? Christie likes him more and more. I can tell. Will she think I'm just jealous and possessive and don't want anyone to go with Keith? Will she be mad at me?

Just then the door to Bumpers opened and some of the football players came in. Trailing behind were Keith and Christie. They were laughing happily.

CHAPTER

*C*hristie took Keith by the hand and led him to the booth where the rest of The Fabulous Five was sitting. Beth stiffened her back and took a deep breath. I can do it, she thought. I can hide my feelings. It's just like acting. All I have to do is concentrate.

"Hi, everybody," Christie said cheerfully.

Keith gave Beth a small smile.

"You don't have room for us," Christie said, looking around for another place to sit.

In a flash Beth said, "I'm leaving. The two of you can squeeze in."

"Oh," said Christie. "Are you sure?"

"I've got to look over my part for tomorrow and

study." Beth was proud of the way she kept her voice from quivering. But it would be better if she left now.

"We're all going to meet at the movies, right?" asked Christie.

"I can't wait to see who this fabulous date of Beth's is," said Melanie.

Beth felt like shrinking down to a little blob. Not only did she not have a date for the movies, but everyone, including Keith, was going to find out that she never had one.

She looked at the other members of The Fabulous Five and gave them a big smile. "Good-bye, everyone." They all smiled back. She had them fooled. She had them all fooled, even Keith. But they would all know the truth tomorrow night.

Play practice went much more smoothly the next day. Mr. Levine was all smiles after Beth finished her big part, and Chet Miller told her what a super job she had done. It had taken a lot of concentration, but she had done it, and she loved every minute of it.

She was starting to like Chet very much. He wasn't like a lot of ninth-graders who thought it beneath their dignity to talk to a seventh-grader. And he was nice looking.

Suddenly an idea struck Beth. She looked at Chet as he was picking up his things to leave. Maybe . . .

Could she be so lucky? She grabbed her books and followed him out of the auditorium.

"You're a super actor," she said as she caught up with him. "Have you been in a lot of plays?"

"Thanks. I've been in several," he answered.

"One of the books I have on acting says you should go to as many movies as possible and analyze them. Do you ever do that?"

He looked at her curiously. "No. I never thought about it."

"Like the movie that's on at the theater tonight. It's supposed to be a good one to study. Are you going?"

"Yeah. I heard it's a riot."

"I suppose you have a date."

"No. I told Jay Chisholm I'd meet him there."

"Oh." Everything was going great. Now if she could just pull off the next part.

"I was thinking about going, but I can't get a ride. My brother's got the car and it would be out of his way."

"Uh"—she took a deep breath before she continued—"you don't suppose I could get a ride with you, do you?"

"Oh, sure. I suppose so. Where do you live?"

Beth almost squealed with delight.

There were lots of kids in front of the theater when Chet's mother and father pulled up to the curb to drop them off. Beth saw The Fabulous Five and

The Fantastic Foursome as well as nearly everyone else she knew that counted.

"Oh, Chet," she said as they got out of the car. "Could you do me a favor and get a ticket for me? I want to say hello to someone." She handed him the money she had been holding since they had picked her up.

"Sure."

She walked with him to the ticket line so everyone could see that she had come with him. Smiling, she waved at Jana, Melanie, Katie, and Christie, who were waiting for their dates to buy tickets.

"I'll be right back," she said, patting Chet on the arm.

"Wow!" said Katie. "Chet Miller."

"And a ninth-grader," said Melanie. "How did you pull that off?"

"Oh, we were just talking after one of our practices," said Beth, leaving out the fact that it had been that day's practice, "and he said he'd pick me up. He's nice."

"We won't be able to sit with you guys, though. Chet wants to sit with Jay Chisholm. I'll see you later." She left them standing with their mouths open, and she could feel the eyes of Laura McCall and The Fantastic Foursome following her, too.

Chet was getting the tickets when she came back, and she went to stand next to him. She saw Keith watching her. He had a strange look on his face.

Luck was still with her when they went inside. They found three seats together. Beth had visualized the ultimate horror of having to sit by herself after she had made everyone think she was going with Chet.

She turned around to see where her friends were sitting, and she looked Keith right in the eyes. They were three rows behind her. He looked away quickly.

After the movie, she stood on the sidewalk with Chet waiting for his parents. All the seventh-grade girls who passed looked at Chet and then at her with envy in their eyes.

"Chet, would your mom and dad mind dropping me off at home, instead of Bumpers?" asked Beth. "I'm not feeling too well." Even though Beth's plan had gone off without a hitch, she didn't want to take any more chances. If she went to Bumpers, someone was bound to say something about their being on a date in front of Chet and ruin everything.

"No, my parents won't mind," Chet said, looking at her closely. "Are you all right?"

He was nice. If she didn't like Keith so much, it would be super to go on a real date with him some-time. That is if he ever really would consider dating a seventh-grade girl.

She smiled at him and nodded. Even though he didn't know it, he had done all he could for her.

CHAPTER

17

"*H*ow in the world did you get a date with Chet Miller?" asked Dekeisha Adams the next afternoon as the cheerleaders gathered in front of the stands before the game.

"He's in ninth grade and everything," Mandy McDermott said with admiration in her voice. "Are you going together now?"

"Oh, no," Beth answered, trying to sound casual. "Just because I went to the movies with him once doesn't mean we're going steady. Who knows if we'll ever go out again?" She thought it was better to eliminate any impressions that they were dating regularly. Her luck had taken her just about as far as it could. She did enjoy the poison-dart looks Laura McCall was giving her over all the attention she was getting from the other cheerleaders.

The stadium was filled, and the Wakeman and Jefferson teams were lined up for the kickoff. Keith was playing back to receive the ball, and Beth couldn't help thinking how much like a Roman warrior he looked with his uniform and helmet.

Today was his last chance to take the lead in rushing. She gave a little silent cheer that he would. He wanted it so badly and had worked so hard for it. He deserved it.

The game was even until the second quarter when Randy Kirwan handed the ball off to Keith, and he burst through the Jefferson line. Two tacklers piled on him, but someway he shook them loose and broke into the open field, running for the first touchdown of the game. The half ended with Wakeman ahead seven to nothing.

During halftime, an announcement came over the speaker. *"Keith Masterson gained thirty-eight yards in the first half. That puts him forty-five yards behind Mike Saharis of Georgetown for the league rushing title."*

"YEA!" yelled all the cheerleaders.

"Let's do He's Our Man," yelled Kaci Davis.

Beth lined up with the others.

"Keith Masterson
He's our man.
He can do it,
if anyone can.
Yeah, Keith!"

Beth felt a swelling of pride as the Wakeman kids cheered for Keith. He would do it. She just knew he would.

In the second half, the Wakeman Warriors pulled further ahead. Keith ground out yards to the left and to the right, and then he would crash into the middle of the line and come out on the other side with players hanging all over him. Once or twice when he got up, she thought he looked in her direction.

"The unofficial count for Keith Masterson is seventy-three yards," came the announcement over the public address system at the end of the third quarter. *"He needs ten more for the rushing title."*

Beth jumped up and down. "Only ten more yards and he's got it," she yelled at Melanie, and pounded on her.

The fourth quarter started. Randy threw a pass to Shane Arrington, and Shane was tackled right in front of the cheerleaders. He got up smiling.

"That one was for Igor," he yelled at the girls. Beth smiled. Shane was always talking about his pet iguana.

On the next play, Keith came through the line and headed right at the cheerleaders, trying to escape four Jefferson players. They trapped him along the sideline and he rammed into them headfirst. Beth gasped as his legs churned and he tried to drive them back, and then she heard a sickening *SNAP*, and he went down.

Beth stood stunned as she watched the agony on Keith's face as he lay writhing and clutching his right leg on the ground in front of her.

"NO!" she screamed, and ran to him.

She fell to her knees with tears streaming down her face.

"Keith! Don't move!" She tried to hold his leg so he couldn't move it. Her stomach lurched, and she felt sick at the sight of it bent at a crazy angle.

"Don't move him! Don't move him!" Coach Bledsoe yelled as he came running up. Others joined them and someone got a doctor who straightened Keith's leg and put him on a stretcher.

Keith looked up at Beth and smiled as they started to carry him away. She took his hand and held it tightly and walked along beside him as they took him off the field. Tears were streaming down her face, but she didn't care at all.

As they passed through the crowd on the way to the parking lot, kids yelled, "Hang in there, Keith!"

and "Tough it out, guy!" She squeezed his hand, and he squeezed back.

Then she saw The Fabulous Five. They all had tears in their eyes. Jana and Katie were looking at Keith, but Christie was watching Beth, and she was crying the most.

CHAPTER

18

Beth sat in the hospital hallway with Mr. and Mrs. Masterson waiting for news about Keith. The paramedics had let her ride in the ambulance, and she had held his hand all the way. His mother and father had been at the game and were only minutes behind in their own car.

The doors at the end of the hall opened, and Jana, Katie, Christie, and Melanie filed in quietly.

"How is Keith?" asked Jana.

"It's his leg. I heard it break," Beth said, grimacing. Her eyes filled with tears again as she remembered the terrible sound.

110

"The doctor hasn't come out of the operating room yet, so we don't know how bad it is."

"I know it's not much consolation," said Katie, "but the announcer said over the loudspeaker that Keith got the yards he needed to go ahead of Mike Saharis with that last run."

"I don't believe he's going to be thinking much about that right now," said Christie, staring at Beth.

They found seats on a bench and sat down to wait.

"Beth, can I talk to you for a minute?" asked Christie. She walked down the hall away from the others and stopped. Beth followed her.

"Can you ever forgive me?" asked Christie, her eyes turning moist. "I didn't know you still liked Keith, honest I didn't. When I saw you holding his hand when he was hurt and walking out with him, I realized how dumb I had been. I thought it was all over between you and him. I wouldn't have gone out with him if I had known." Christie's voice caught, and Beth saw she was about to break out in tears.

Beth reached out and put her arms around her. "It was my fault. I said those dumb things about not wanting to go with him anymore because I was mad at him, and then I didn't know how to take them back. But what was worse, I played the big actress and kept my real feelings hidden instead of being honest. I'm not mad at you."

"Not just a little bit for not realizing what was going on?"

Beth smiled. "Well, maybe I was a little bit, but I'm not anymore. I know it was just all a big misunderstanding. Besides, Keith has terrific taste in girls."

Christie sniffed and hugged Beth back. "Friends forever?" she asked.

Beth smiled. "Friends forever."

The elevator doors opened and a doctor came out with a surgical mask hanging from his neck.

"Mr. and Mrs. Masterson?" he asked, walking toward them. They all got up quickly.

"First, let me assure you that Keith's going to be fine. He'll be able to get around okay and should be out of the hospital in a day or two. You might want to make arrangements to get his homework from school, however, since he'll be staying home for a couple of weeks. If you want to go up and see him, you can, but I wouldn't recommend all of you going. He's still pretty groggy from the anesthesia."

"I think Beth should go with Mr. and Mrs. Masterson," said Christie. The others agreed.

The room smelled like antiseptic, and Keith's leg was suspended in the air. He smiled weakly when he saw them.

"Hi, champ," said Mr. Masterson. "How's it going?" Keith's mother bent over and kissed him.

"Not too great," answered Keith. "Did I get the yards I needed?"

"You got them," said Beth.

His smile grew bigger.

They had been talking for only a few minutes when a nurse came into the room. "I'm sorry to interrupt, but I need some additional insurance information. Could you help me with it, please?"

"Sure," said Keith's father. His mother went with them into the hall.

Beth stepped up to Keith's bed.

"Hi," he said, giving her one of his special smiles.

"Hi. I heard that you're going to be out of school for a couple of weeks and will need someone to bring your assignments home. I'll do it. And if you need someone to study with, that's me."

"I appreciate it, but you'll be too busy."

"No, I won't," she said softly. "I've decided to drop out of the school play. I'll have lots of time."

"Drop out of the school play?" Surprise spread across his face. "Why?"

"Oh . . . it's taking too much time, and it's no big deal."

He looked at her a moment. "I don't think you should."

It was her turn to be surprised at him. He had

been the one who thought it would take up too much of her time before. Why would he change his mind?

"You really do like acting, Beth. I know you do. Are you just saying you'll drop out because of me?"

She lowered her eyes, not knowing how to answer.

"Hey," he said, frowning at her. "With this leg I'm not going to be playing sports for a while. Now I think I know how you felt when I was hassling you not to try out for the play so you could spend more time with me. I guess I never thought about how badly I wanted to play sports until all of a sudden I couldn't. It wouldn't be fair for you to drop out of the play for me. You want to act as badly as I want to play football or basketball."

He looked at her closely. "Let me ask you something. Why would you drop out of the play for me anyway? I thought you weren't interested in going with me anymore."

"I was just mad at you," she said.

"The way you acted, I thought you didn't want to date me at all."

"I'm an actress, remember. I can make all kinds of things seem different from what they really are. I just imagine I'm a certain person or I feel a certain way, and it's that way."

"Well, don't act that well again," he said, reaching his hand out for hers.

Beth stood in the center of the stage and listened to the applause. It was the first night of the play, and it had been a major success.

She looked into the wings, and Mr. Levine was smiling broadly at her and pointing to the front row where Mr. Stapleton was standing and clapping enthusiastically.

She could also see her mother and father, Brian, Brittany, Todd, and Alicia about four rows back. Everyone in the family had come to see the show except Agatha.

Farther back were The Fabulous Five, applauding as hard as they could and making thumbs-up signs. And standing in the aisle with a cast that went from his ankle to above his knee, was Keith. He was applauding loudest of all. Beth thought she could actually hear him above all the rest. She gave him her special smile.

Keith stood behind the center. "Ready! Set! Hut!" he called the signals, and the ball was snapped.

He grabbed it and hobbled to the right looking for his receiver.

"Throw it!" yelled Todd, backing up and falling over Agatha.

Beth dashed in and caught Keith around the waist, pulling him down. He was easy.

"You got me," he said, laughing.

"It's not fair," said Todd. "Agatha tripped me."

"You have to look out for those free safeties," kidded Keith.

"Agafa's not free," said Alicia. Beth and Keith both laughed.

Beth got up and held out her hands for him to hold on to as he struggled with his cast.

"The stick! The stick!" Keith said with a grimace.

Beth got the long, thin stick that Keith carried with him everywhere nowadays.

He grabbed it and slid it down inside the cast and moved it up and down in a scratching motion.

"Oooh," he said with a silly smile on his face. "That was a bad itch."

"From the look on your face, I'd think it's almost worth it to have an itch like that so you can scratch it."

"Not so," he said, pulling the stick out again.

She put her arm around his waist as they walked to the door. "Can I ask you something?"

"Sure," he said.

"When you were dating Christie, I wondered about a few things."

"Like what?"

"Do you think Christie is prettier than me?"

He looked at her, and she could see that he was having a hard time holding back a smile.

"Does she kiss as good as me?" she continued.

"Maybe," he answered.

She punched him in the ribs.

"Ooof! Hey, you almost knocked the wind out of me. Remember, I'm crippled."

"Well, you got the answer wrong."

"I don't think there is a right answer to your last question. If I said she doesn't kiss as good as you, you'll be mad because I kissed her at all. If I said she kisses better than you, I'm dead."

Beth giggled. "Maybe my question *wasn't* fair."

"What did Mr. Stapleton say to you when you talked to him?" Keith asked.

"Oh, he had some suggestions about ways I could improve, and he told me that when he teaches acting somewhere around here, he'd like to see me in his class."

She thought for a minute before she asked her next question. "Do you feel really bad about not being able to play sports for a while?

"I'm not happy about it," he answered. "But maybe it will help out my grades."

"You could take up acting," she suggested.

"Hmm. I think one of us being an actor is enough."

"Maybe," she said, putting her arms around his neck. "Just maybe."

CHAPTER

"*I*'m really glad that you and Keith are back together," Jana said to Beth a few days later as they left school together. "I really felt bad when the two of you were having problems."

Beth gave her an appreciative smile. "So did I. You know, sometimes I look at you and Randy and wish Keith and I had such a smooth relationship as you two do."

Jana linked arms with her best friend as they walked along, trying not to grin. What did Beth expect? she wondered. Beth had a wild and crazy personality, and her flair for drama kept her entire life from being anything but smooth. Still, Beth had a point.

"I know what you mean," Jana mused. "Sometimes I wonder myself just how Randy and I manage to avoid major problems. We almost never fight. It's really sort of weird."

"Don't knock it," said Beth with a laugh. "The only good part about breaking up is getting back together."

Jana gave Beth an understanding nod as they went into Bumpers and joined the rest of The Fabulous Five at a table. Jana tried to join in the conversation as her friends chattered loudly to make themselves heard above the noisy crowd, but she couldn't shake off an eerie feeling that had come over her during her conversation with Beth. It was as dark and scary as the shadow made by a cloud passing over the moon. She shivered and tried to make the feeling go away, but it wouldn't. No matter how hard she tried, she couldn't stop herself from thinking that something terrible was going to happen between Randy and her.

Will Jana's premonition come true? Or is she only letting her imagination get the best of her? Find out in *The Fabulous Five #11: Hit and Run.*

ABOUT THE AUTHOR

Betsy Haynes, the daughter of a former news-woman, began scribbling poetry and short stories as soon as she learned to write. A serious writing career, however, had to wait until after her marriage and the arrival of her two children. But that early practice must have paid off, for within three months Mrs. Haynes had sold her first story. In addition to a number of magazine short stories and the Taffy Sinclair series, Mrs. Haynes is also the author of *The Great Mom Swap* and its sequel, *The Great Boyfriend Trap*. She lives in Colleyville, Texas, with her husband, who is also an author.

Great FREE offer just for you!

Join SNEAK PEEKS™!

Do you want to know what's new before anyone else? Do you like to read great books about girls just like you? If you do, then you won't want to miss SNEAK PEEKS™! Be the first of your friends to know what's hot ... When you join SNEAK PEEKS™, we'll send you FREE inside information in the mail about the latest books ... *before they're published!* Plus updates on your favorite series, authors, and exciting new stories filled with friendship and fun ... adventure and mystery ... girlfriends and boyfriends.

It's easy to be a member of SNEAK PEEKS™. Just fill out the coupon below ... and get ready for fun! It's FREE! Don't delay—sign up today!